Back Co

Two tiger shifters struggle to find their way past pain and heartbreak in the hopes of discovering their own happily ever after.

Belle lives in a village that is a sanctuary for feline shifters who need a place to escape their troubles and start anew. She's a tiger shifter and the only female enforcer for the small community—a position that fills her with pride. She's happy and content with her life, although her mother has been badgering her about finding a mate. But as far as Belle is concerned, if her mate wants her, he can come seek her out.

Things begin to change when their Alpha gives approval for Shawn, a male tiger shifter, to become part of their community. Belle instantly knows he's her mate. But he's spent years in a violent relationship. He's tired, his self-confidence has disappeared, and he's extremely leery of getting involved again.

Then tragedy strikes and suddenly Belle is dealing with her own heartbreak. Meanwhile, Shawn is still struggling to escape his past, dealing with a vengeful ex and city police who seem to believe he was the abuser rather than the victim.

Can these two shifters overcome all the obstacles blocking the path to true love?

Content Warning: contains strong language, some violence, and lots of hot, steamy sex scenes

Chapter 1

Shawn Burr walked into his office and placed the two styrofoam cups of coffee on his desk. Removing his coat, he hung it up just as his boss called his name. Sighing, he picked up one of the cups and walked down the small hallway leading to his boss's office, knowing the look he was about to get.

Paul's eyebrows rose in surprise, then he shook his head in dismay. "Again?" he asked. "How many *accidents* has this been this month?" He said the word *accidents* with a cynical tone. "And just how hard did she hit you this time to need that?" Paul pointed to the bandage on Shawn's head.

Shawn lifted his hand, touching the bandage on his brow. Both Paul and Shawn were shifters—Shawn was a tiger, and Paul was a wolf—and they healed faster than the average human. But the wound Rosie had inflicted last night had been so bad it had required stitches. That should have told him just how abusive things had gotten, and yet there he was in front of his friend and boss ready to justify why Rosie, his fiancée, had turned on him again last night.

Shawn and Rosie had been together since the end of college. They'd met in a bar; she was celebrating getting a job as the assistant manager at the huge hotel in town. She was carefree and fun in the beginning of their relationship, but as her job began taking its toll she brought her grievances home with her.

Rosie was the youngest of six children. Her siblings were all male, and she had learned from a young age how to take care of herself. Shawn quickly found out just how well she could do that. She was able to manipulate her brothers; she had each of them wrapped around her little finger. Having five burly siblings at her beck and call had boosted her ego and given her the impression that the world should bow down at her.

Shawn and Rosie had been involved for four years now, and between the embarrassment and fear that her brothers would track him down, he put up with Rosie's attitude and abuse. No one but Paul knew what went on behind closed doors. Even the few friends he'd had were now non-existent.

As a shifter, Shawn was exceptional at keeping secrets, but his tiger had been very quiet for about two years now. The other half of his soul didn't agree with letting a female treat Shawn the way she did. He had urged Shawn to leave Rosie and go look for their true mate, the woman who would love and care for them until the end of time. Shawn had felt the loss of his other half greatly. The last year had been worse. He had never felt so alone in the world as he did now.

He'd grown up with loving parents who had spent years on the run after their own pack disallowed their mating. Not long after Shawn had left college, his parents were killed in a drive-by shooting. To this day Shawn didn't know if the bullets were meant for them or if they'd merely been in the wrong place at the wrong time. He'd met Rosie a few months after that, and she'd helped with the sorrow he felt.

He knew she wasn't his true mate, but over time their love grew, and he'd been willing to imprint on Rosie enough to forget his true mate could be out there. His tiger didn't agree and hated the woman and her treatment enough to retreat far into Shawn's mind and stay there.

"Paul…" Shawn walked to his desk and placed Paul's coffee down.

"Don't *Paul* me. You think I don't know what's going on? I'm not stupid you know. You can get help."

Shawn knew how angry Paul was because his eyes kept flashing between amber and blue. The man's wolf was so close to the surface it seemed to be fighting to get out.

"She's just having a hard time at the moment." Shawn tried to reason with his friend and boss.

"She's been having a hard time for what, a year now? Two?" he asked, slapping his hands on the desk. He took a deep breath and exhaled loudly. "I can't help unless you ask for it."

Paul shook his head and waved his hand, shooing Shawn out of his office in exasperation. Shawn walked out of the office, his hand on the doorknob, ready to close it when Paul yet again offered his never ending support.

"I'm here when you need me, Shawn. I just hope you accept my help before she kills you."

Nodding, Shawn pulled the door shut and walked to his desk. Sitting down, he asked himself the same questions he'd been asking himself for a while. Did he love Rosie enough to stay with her any longer? Where would he go if he left? He had no family to turn to, to gather help from. What would he do? Who would believe him anyway? Could he stay hidden enough to escape her brothers? Sighing, he pushed the thoughts away and turned his mind to work.

Shawn had worked for Paul Hardy as a receptionist and PA for four years. Shawn had management skills thanks to several courses he'd taken in college, but he had known since childhood that he wasn't interested in being a millionaire, high roller type of person. He loved helping people, and he enjoyed his work. He met many different people through his job. Shawn's boss was a solicitor. He wasn't one of those rich, high society people either—he handled a lot of cases through legal aid. Shawn's job could be challenging. Every day was different, even if the paperwork was the same.

He'd been ridiculed by some of his friends in the beginning…a receptionist? But he would shrug his shoulders. Not everyone wanted to be a manager, lawyer, or something high class, and he was happy doing his job.

The day flew by. Several meetings and a whole lot of filing kept him busy, and it wasn't until he noticed the dimming light that he looked up and took notice of the time. *Shit!* Standing, he grabbed his coat, called out to Paul that he was leaving, and ran to the car park. Rosie didn't like it when he was late.

"You're a receptionist, a nine-to-five job, there is no reason for you to be late. I'm a fucking manager. I'm the one who works all hours. You're supposed to be here ready and waiting when I get home," she would scream.

As he drove down the motorway, he knew tonight there would be hell…again. Every time she got angry, he would take it. Each time she threw something at him he would justify it. Any time she laid a hand on him, he thought he deserved it. Afterward she always cried and apologized profusely, saying she wouldn't do it again. She would arrive home with a present of some sort the next day. For a few days after things would be great, but then he'd go and do something wrong again in her eyes.

But he was growing tired of being her battering post, her apologies became meaningless, and he was beginning to realize she wasn't going to change. The threat of her brothers coming after him if he left her was beginning to lose its effectiveness, and it was becoming more and more tempting to find out if they would. What was the worst they could do? Kill him? Bring him back? Being brought back would be worse than death.

He often wondered what Rosie would do if he told her about his tiger. She had no idea Shawn was a shifter. It was the one thing he had kept hidden from his volatile fiancée. The shifter world was a secret, but as a potential person Shawn might imprint on, a future mate, he could tell her. Shawn knew if he told her, it could go either way, good or bad. She could be freaked out enough to leave him or she could be manipulative enough to blackmail him with it. In a way he was glad that he hadn't opened that door.

There was no way on this earth he would ever raise a hand to a woman. He'd thought about going to the police once or twice after she'd hit him, but with his fast healing his bruises would quickly disappear. When the injuries hadn't healed quickly, like last night, as he sat in the hospital waiting for stitches for the umpteenth time, he wondered how he could explain it so that someone believed him. He wouldn't have a leg to stand on, because who would believe a two hundred pound, six-foot man was being abused by his five-foot fiancée? Her brothers would be behind her all the way; they made escaping her just as hard. The first time he'd met them, they'd encircled him and threatened bodily harm if he ever laid a finger on her.

Shawn turned onto a suburban street just outside Yorkshire and pulled up in front of a three-bedroom house with a white picket fence. In spring and summer it was covered in flowers, portraying the picture of a happy family home. When Rosie received her promotion to manager two years ago, she had dragged him house hunting with her. When she'd seen this place she'd fallen in love with it. A week after the deeds had been signed they had moved in. He'd gone along with it, because he would do anything to see her happy. So why tonight as he drove up the driveway did he feel dread in his heart? Why did he feel sick to the very depths of his stomach? The sight of the house now brought nothing but misery. Fear rode him hard. For a few seconds he actually thought about turning his car around and leaving, but then the front door opened and Rosie stood in the doorway with her hands on her hips. *Crap!*

He got out of the car, and before he even made it inside the house Rosie was yelling. "Why are you late? Are you seeing someone else?" Her hands roamed his body as if looking for evidence of an affair.

Turning his back to her, he placed his coat on the coat rack near the door. "I forgot the time. I'm sorry, work was busy today." He held up his hands, trying to appease her.

The sound of skin slapping on skin rang out loud, and Shawn's head whipped to the side. Pain shot through his cheek. He turned his head back to Rosie, raising his hand to the burning sensation she had left behind with her palm.

"Why?" he asked. He wasn't surprised she'd hit him, but for some reason he wanted to hear her feeble excuse for doing so.

"I am the fucking manager. I'm the one who fucking works long hours. You are supposed to be home before me and greet *me* at the door!" Rosie turned away from him and stomped into the kitchen.

Inhaling a slow, deep breath, he followed. "I'm sorry, honey. I'll try to keep better track of the time. I don't do it often. It was a mistake."

She sat down at the kitchen table and pulled a large glass of wine in front of her, indicating she was done. Sighing to himself, Shawn started pulling stuff out of the fridge for dinner. He knew keeping his mouth shut at this stage was the best idea.

"Stuffed mushrooms?" he asked with his back to her, hiding his grimace and hoping he'd guessed right for the meal.

"Fine," she grumbled. Standing, she walked out of the room with her wine glass in hand.

Shawn blew out a breath. It looked like he'd gotten off easy tonight. He cooked for the next hour or so, enjoying the peace. But just as he was dishing up the food a raging, red-faced Rosie stormed into the kitchen.

"Men! You just don't seem to understand, do you?"

His hand which was holding a set of tongs stalled in the air. He quickly ran through everything he'd done in the house that morning until now. Towel on the rack and not on the floor. Had he placed the cap back on the toothpaste? Had he made the bed? He was sure he hadn't left the toilet seat up.

Gingerly, he asked, "Uh, honey, what's up?"

"What's up?" she shrieked. "What the fuck is up?" she screamed louder and began pacing up and down in short, quick, jerky movements. "A few things have gone missing at work, so the owner asked for a stock report. I ordered Phil, the deputy manager, to do a stock intake. He forgot. He fucking forgot, and tonight I get the owner of the hotel asking me for the list. One fucking blunder and I get it in the neck. It wasn't even my doing. Ahhh!" Rosie screamed and threw the empty glass she held in her hand. It went flying across the room. Tinkering shards of glass as it shattered across the kitchen floor could be heard before Rosie screamed again. "Why can't things go right?"

Shawn placed the tongs on the counter carefully, trying not to make a sound, knowing full well any little movement or sound right now would turn her anger onto him. His tiger inside of him stirred, growled deeply, and then curled itself up in a tighter ball and went back to sleep. Shawn jolted, feeling a huge loss and rejection yet again. He wanted so badly to be in touch with his lifelong friend again. Any kind of support from anyone would be a dream at this precise moment.

Why was he doing this? Why had he let Rosie treat him like shit for so long? He hadn't even shared his tiger with her in the years they'd been together. Wasn't that how relationships were supposed to work? He longed to share that with a mate, to have kits with one. Just to be happy and comfortable.

The tongs rocked from side to side. With silent dread Shawn looked up, straight into the wild eyes of his fiancée. He knew in that second that no matter what he did, who he was, it wasn't him that would make Rosie or himself happy.

Here it comes was his last thought before all hell broke loose. Rosie lost it. Her face turned red and she started screaming, shouting, and thrashing at him with her fists and feet. When he tried to hold her off by grabbing her wrists, she screeched louder.

"Want to hit me, do you? Well, come on, big boy, here's your chance, hit a woman!"

He instantly let go of her wrists, guilt wracking him. He would never harm her, no matter what she did. He saw her pick up the pan he'd been boiling green beans in and watched as she pitched it toward him. Instinctively, his arms rose to protect his face. The water rolled down his forearms, his skin burning and stinging. Pain filled every pore in his limbs.

"I'm sorry, Rosie, but it isn't my fault." His begging voice came out, muffled behind his arms. He lowered them a fraction to look over his hands to see what she was doing only to feel more pain. *Smack!* The pan flashed right across the side of his face.

He didn't dare move. He stood stiff as a post, his arms again raised in front of his face, his teeth biting down on his tongue to keep quiet through the pain. The sound of the pan being dropped to the floor left him waiting to see what came next. Nothing.

Gradually, he dropped his arms and watched in stunned silence as Rosie, his once blonde goddess whom he had loved with all his heart and soul, grabbed a chopping knife off the counter and plunged it into his stomach before he could even think about defending himself.

Seeing the anger she directed at him, his heart broke, and tears filled his eyes. As the world dulled in roaring pain he cried out to his tiger, wanting his companion to love him one last time. His knees collapsed underneath him as pain racked his body. He looked down between his linked fingers to see his blood pouring through them. So this was how it was to end? Paul had only just said that morning he hoped Shawn asked for help before she killed him.

Cold seeped into his veins as more blood left his body. Falling onto his side, he curled up into a ball. The pain slowly seemed to drift away. *That isn't a good thing.* Closing his eyes, he again searched his mind to find his lifelong companion and curled up along its side. When his tiger purred and curled up with him he almost felt like crying, but he didn't have the energy.

Shawn had no idea how long he lay there flitting in and out of oblivion. Memories of what happened slowly seeped back each time he became conscious. Every time he remembered, he looked around in panic, trying to see or hear Rosie. But from what he could tell, she wasn't there.

His hands were clutched to his stomach, and he could feel the warm liquid of life seeping through his fingers. Again he asked himself how he could have let a woman beat the living shit out of him. Who in the world would believe that? He was just about to close his eyes again and give up when he heard the faint sound of a siren in the distance growing closer. Was that for him? Did he care?

The next time he opened his eyes he saw the face of a paramedic leaning over him and telling him he was going to be okay. At that point he didn't care. He closed his eyes and curled up tighter with his beast. Inwardly, he cried when his tiger woke up beside him and roared, then it quietly nudged its head under Shawn's chin and purred.

Chapter 2

Belle Grant grunted, feeling the bone-jarring jolt as her back hit the ground.

"Hey, no fair, Felix. You cheated."

"No, woman." He chuckled. "You should have been ready."

"Just because I asked to be under you on the enforcers' team instead of Barry's team, doesn't mean I want to be *under* you."

Felix laughed, and bent over, placing his hands on his knees. Belle flipped up and landed on her feet, then sideswiped her right foot, kicking out just below Felix's knee. The sound of a crack rang out, then Felix landed on his butt with a groan.

"Hey!" he yelled.

"Should have been ready." She threw his words back at him.

"Har de fucking har." He sighed. "Okay, you win." Instead of flipping himself up, he held his hand out for her to pull him up. "I'm not looking for someone to be *under* me," he said as she yanked him up. "I'm looking for someone to take over for me while I'm out of town."

"You finally have enough cash to go on your trip?"

He smiled from ear to ear and nodded. Everyone in the small town knew Felix was desperate to go sow his wild oats elsewhere. He'd gone through the majority of the women in the village, Belle not being one of them. Even with his outstanding body and charming and comical personality, she hadn't fallen for him. One thing no one knew about her was she wanted to wait for her mate, to give him the part of herself she wouldn't give to another—her virginity. Felix had instead become her best friend.

"Yeah, and Harris is grumbling about it. Sometimes I think he still sees me as a kid. It's even worse for Terrie."

"He'll get over it. He has his own son now."

"You would think, right?" Felix sighed. "Since Walker was born, I swear my brother has become more protective. He's even put fellow enforcer Larry on Terrie's tail at all times. She didn't take that very well. She's still sulking seven months later."

"I can see that girl wanting to do her own backpacking soon." Belle laughed. She loved Terrie like a sister. Terrie was incredibly spunky, and Belle wished she'd been like the young woman at her age. "Is Harris okay with me taking over as beta until you get back?"

"Yeah, although he was put out a bit. He doesn't like taking you off Melinda's protection team, but he admitted he couldn't imagine anyone else who would be a better beta."

Belle felt pride in that statement. She'd never thought of treading in Felix's shoes as beta. Over the last year, ever since Belle had been put on protection duty for Melinda, Harris's mate, she'd grown quite close to the alpha female, and she knew she would miss being at her side.

Belle had been quiet as a teen. She hadn't had the normal fine-tuned, muscled body of a teenage shifter. She knew what it was like to be picked on and challenged every day while in school. Even now, at twenty-nine years old, she was still on the chubbier side for a shifter. She had ample curves, but in truth, she liked it. She didn't want a body with bones jutting out all over the place…it looked painful. Plus, she knew she had boobs to die for, boobs the males looked at before her face. She found it enjoyable to embarrass a male for doing so.

Belle had grown up in the small village of Stonesdale, a place a wise feline shifter had set up as a sanctuary a few hundred years ago. The village was now filled with different kinds of feline shifters from bobcats to the snow leopards the Alpha and his siblings were. They lived happily together in peace and harmony.

Thirty years ago her father, who was a tiger shifter, had been kicked out of his pride, his Alpha deeming him a threat to his own leadership. With nowhere to go, he came across Stonesdale, and there he met his mate. He instantly applied to join the community. After receiving the Alpha's approval, he had gratefully moved into the village and set up home with his mate. They settled down and enjoyed family life. Although they had planned for a whole family of kits, Belle had been the only kit to come along. She was very close to her parents. Even after joining the enforcers, and at the age of twenty-nine, she still lived with her parents.

"So?" Felix said, asking a question with one word.

She searched her mind, trying to remember what they were talking about before her mind ran away onto other things. "So…" she repeated.

"Would you be willing to take over beta duties until I return?"

Her heart swelled. She couldn't, and wouldn't, even think

about refusing. Even if she were to meet her mate tomorrow—which the chances of that happening were slim given that no male in the village had yet appealed to her or her tiger—she would make sure she would make her parents and Alpha proud.

"What about Chris?" she asked, thinking of an older male who she thought might be a tad better than she was for the position.

"I haven't asked him," Felix said with a growing blush on his cheeks. "To be honest, you were the first I thought of. Even for a female you know the ins and outs of the team's shit."

"For a female, huh?" She bent her left knee, swiped out with her right leg, and watched Felix hit the floor with a jolt. "Catch you later, pussy cat."

She laughed, heading toward the Alpha's house. She'd given Felix the nickname *pussy cat* after learning that when Melinda had been told about shifters she had thought they turned into tiny house cats. The nickname did what Belle intended for it to do—it annoyed Felix.

Today she was again on protection duty for Melinda and Walker. Harris wasn't going to be around; he had to meet a male who needed an emergency placement.

"I'll make you pay for that in tomorrow morning's training," Felix shouted out to her.

Yeah, yeah, she thought. Both she and her tiger couldn't wait to experience that.

* * * *

"Mr. Burr?"

Shawn lifted his head from his hospital bed to look at the nurse who was standing by the doorway of his room. He could also see the fully uniformed copper guarding his door.

"There's a visitor here to see you. He says you're expecting him."

"Yes, you can send him in. Thank you," Shawn replied.

He looked around the room where he'd been for the last three days. The sight of those hospital walls made him feel more and more depressed every time he looked at them. He'd been told he was lucky to be found when he had been. A neighbor had heard the screaming and shouting and grew concerned. He'd telephoned the police and ambulance when he saw Rosie run out of the house with bloody hands, leaving the front door wide open.

Shawn had spent several hours in surgery. When he'd woken up and was able to speak, he was interviewed by the police. He had seen the total disbelief in their eyes at first, which made him feel weak, stupid, and worthless. It wasn't until Paul showed up and added his side to it that things turned around and the police began treating Shawn like a victim and not a criminal.

Rosie had yet to be found. To make matters sink in further, someone had sent a bunch of black roses to his room. Attached to them was a card with a face on it, and in place of the mouth was a zipper. The police had taken the flowers and card away as evidence, but Shawn got the message loud and clear.

After that, Paul sat down with Shawn and told him about a little village in Yorkshire. He explained that the small community was run by an Alpha named Harris Rockwell—a snow leopard. It was a sanctuary for feline shifters who needed a peaceful place to hang their hats.

Depression quickly crept up on Shawn. Accepting the fact he'd allowed himself to be abused only made it worse. The only comfort he found was inside his head with his tiger. After another night's rest, Shawn relented and agreed to allow Paul to contact Harris. He knew it was time to move on and be the man he wanted to be rather than the mouse he felt like. For the first time in months, his tiger purred deep inside of him and started speaking to him.

About time you opened your eyes. Little female not deserve you, his tiger said inside his head.

I'm sorry, Shawn apologized.

No sorry anymore. I help you be strong again.

Shawn pictured himself curling up with his tiger and purred along with him.

"Mr. Burr?" a deep voice said from the doorway.

Shawn looked in the direction of the voice to see a man that exuded Alpha. Dominant waves rolled off him, which confirmed to Shawn that this man was Harris Rockwell.

"Alpha," Shawn said, dropping his head slightly, his voice low enough that only a shifter would hear.

Harris stepped inside the room alongside another male who looked similar to him. "This is my brother Felix." Harris gestured to the man. "Paul told us you might need a helping hand."

Shawn sighed. He wasn't ready to tell his story yet again.

Each time he had to tell someone he could feel every ounce of masculinity dropping away.

Before he could say anything Harris spoke again. "I can't say I understand exactly what you've been through, but your friend Paul explained as much as he could to me."

Harris lowered himself into the bedside chair and leaned forward, his elbows resting on his knees. His brother stood by the now closed door with his arms across his chest.

"I would still like to hear your story," Harris said. "I'm not here to judge. I'm just here to meet someone who might find our small, safe community somewhere to call home."

Shawn hesitated, looking down at his hands. "I can tell you that at the moment I feel like a stupid idiot, and anything that has to do with being a man has disappeared along with my confidence. I can't believe I let my life turn out the way it did." Tears he hated so much welled in his eyes. *Another display of weakness*, he thought. His tiger roared inside of him.

"We all have our weaknesses," Harris said reassuringly.

"I'm a man." He thumped his chest, feeling angry at his situation. "I'm supposed to be the strong one. I'm the one who is supposed to be fearless. Letting a woman abuse me? Who is going to want me after that? What female will think of me as a proper man when I don't even think it myself?" He let his head drop to his chest. He was fast losing the will to live.

"We share a weakness, my friend. My female has me wrapped around her little finger. I'd die for her."

"Truth?"

"Yeah, he's telling the truth. I have a best friend who calls me 'pussy cat' now 'cause of his mate." Felix motioned to his brother. Shawn's face must have shown the horror he felt about it, because Felix quickly added, "Oh, I don't mind," He chuckled. "I quite like it. But I wouldn't tell her that, because then she'd come up with something I didn't like." Felix grimaced.

Harris shook his head at his brother's comments, then looked toward Shawn. "You just happened to get the bad apple, mate," Harris said, his voice full of sincerity.

Chapter 3

"Why don't you tell me your story, then I'll tell you a little about our community." Harris smiled as he spoke.

Shawn shrank inside himself. The thought of telling his story again made him feel sick.

Give them a chance. We no want to die yet. I here now. I promise I no leave you again. You strong, never hit female when she hit you. His tiger sent a stream of love and reassurance through to him, purring gently inside of him. Shawn could feel the truth in his words.

Nodding slowly, he retold his story again for Harris and his brother. "We met four months after my parents were shot in a drive-by. Things were good in the beginning, but over time things gradually began to change. She would complain things weren't in the right place, toothpaste caps weren't on, towels were not put back—all the general stuff I suppose. One evening after a stressful day at work she threw an ornament at my head. I wrote it off as PMS. As I said, over time it grew worse. The first time she hit me it was with a frying pan. I can't tell you how bloody shocked I was. I remember standing frozen solid, holding my head as she stood in front of me and continued screaming as if she hadn't just belted me around the noggin' with the pan in her hand. I thought about moving out. I knew it wasn't right for her to hit me. But I loved her. There was the fact of her brothers too. They frightened me stupid."

Memories of the first time he met her siblings went through

his mind, making him shudder. Each one of the brothers had made him promise that he would never put a hand on their treasured little sister. He had to promise he would treat her like fragile glass, and they warned him that if he didn't they would make his life hell.

"She was their angel. She's the baby sister to five brothers, so you can imagine that as far as they're concerned, she can't say or do anything wrong. I felt cornered. Who the hell would believe me? I mean look at me, I'm six feet..." He trailed off, tired from having to explain what he'd gone through and why.

Inhaling deeply, he paused a minute, then continued.

"All kinds of things went through my head over the last few years. Did I really deserve it? Was it normal? How could I escape? I again got very close to leaving her two years ago. I'd packed a bag and was about to walk out the door when she walked in. That was a shitty conversation. For the first hour she sat on the sofa crying, begging me not to go. Then came the threats that all our money went into her account, leaving me with nothing. Even my car was in her name. Then she accused me of wanting to leave her for someone else. But yet again, after a few days of crap she apologized profusely, promising to change. Believing her, I agreed to stay. Things were good for about a month, but over time she went right back to being her normal self. She began keeping tabs on me. My phone, my work, and what few friends I had. Eventually even they dropped off the face of the earth. I didn't go anywhere but work and home. Each time she hit me or threw something at me it would tear a little piece of me away. Even my tiger got fed up and curled up, depressed, inside of me. He refused to admit he was part of me until the…until she stabbed me." He whispered the last bit as embarrassment swam through his veins.

Shawn looked up in alarm when Harris let out a small, low growl.

"I'm angry *for* you, not *at* you." Harris shook his head. "I looked into the statistics of your situation before I came. Forty percent of men live in that type of relationship, so you are not alone, friend."

Shawn didn't know what to say.

"I also hear that your ex has not yet been found," Harris said.

Shawn shook his head. "I think her brothers are helping to keep her hidden, but there's no proof of that. An arrest warrant has been issued, but nothing else can be done until she turns up. Did Paul tell you about the flowers I received yesterday?"

Harris nodded. "You've been here for three days, right? Which means you need to leave soon before your shifter healing is discovered and questioned. If I was to offer you a home with us and take you there today, do you have anything to bring with you?"

"You're offering a place in your village?" Shawn asked in surprise. "You believe me? Well, I know you can tell I'm not lying because you can scent it. It's just… I suppose it's been so long since I thought anyone would believe me I'm just shocked. Sorry."

"I wouldn't be asking you if I didn't believe you. A copper would not be standing outside your door if they didn't trust you were telling the truth. And I doubt your boss Paul would have given you a glowing account of character if *he* didn't. So before you go any further, you have to begin to believe it yourself too. You and your tiger have a ways to mend, my friend."

Harris stood and offered Shawn his right hand. It only took Shawn a few seconds before placing his right hand in the Alpha's.

"I, Alpha of Stonesdale sanctuary for feline shifters, am offering you, Shawn Burr, a home. A place where you can be safe from outside conflict."

Tears stung the back of Shawn's eyes. For the first time in three days he felt like he could begin to mend. "Thank you, Alpha. I accept."

* * * *

"Oh crap, he's doing it again," Melinda cried out from the sitting room.

Belle had been walking around checking the house when she heard the tired cry. Rushing to the room where Melinda and her son were, Belle couldn't help but bend over in laughter. Walker was on his feet, trying to climb up and into his high chair again. He wasn't trying to climb in it because he was hungry, he just loved climbing up then jumping off it, knowing his mother would catch him. The little imp had run his mother ragged while his father was away.

Up until the age of five, feline shifter children—kits—developed a lot faster than the average human child. They spoke earlier and walked at around six months. After the age of five, they slowed down physically, but they were mentally more advanced until they hit their teens, that's where their hormones took over, giving human children time to catch up with them. That was one reason the majority of shifter children were taught at home or in the village school. Walker was proving at the age of seven months how fast he was learning to climb. Belle watched Melinda collapse in an exasperated pile on the floor with Walker now held protectively on her chest after he had jumped from his chair.

"Oh God, I can't wait for his father to get home."

"Here," Belle said, going over and picking Walker up. "I'll take him off your hands for half an hour."

With her hands held together as if praying, Melinda whispered, "Thank you." Picking herself up from the floor, Melinda threw herself on the sofa.

"Come on, imp, let's go put your new climbing frame to use."

With an excited "Weeeeee," and his hands held over the top of his head, she whipped him up high and onto her shoulders and went out the back door. As soon as they were standing in front of the frame, Walker took off climbing over the apparatus.

Belle watched the kit play. He looked so much like his father, but he had his mother's eyes. Only this morning Belle's own mother had reminded her that she would turn thirty this year. Her mother had again tried to convince her to go out into the world and see if she could find her mate. Belle had rolled her eyes and sighed, telling her, "I'm happy here. Plus, I don't want to leave you just yet. If fate wants me to find my mate, he will have to look for me here."

Watching Walker play, her tiger moved inside her,

complaining that it too was ready to settle down.

Don't you start, she told the other half of herself.

You know you are ready to settle down too. Look at the boy. You could make you and your mother happy.

I'm not ready to leave them on their own yet. You know how Mum struggles now. If it was meant to be, it will do so here.

Her tiger growled low, and Belle chuckled inwardly.

"*We have incoming,*" Chris, one of their enforcers, alerted her telepathically.

She tensed. "*Details?*" she asked, and went on to inform Chris where she was in case of trouble. "*I'm with Walker and Melinda at the Alpha's house.*"

"*It's okay. It's the Alpha, beta, and the male they said they might be bringing in with them.*"

Belle relaxed. "Melinda," she called. Picking Walker up, she moved toward the house. "Come on, munchkin, let's go see your daddy."

Melinda met them at the back door. "What's up?"

"Harris is back." She smiled at her friend.

"Am I a bad mum to say thank God." She chuckled nervously, then sighed in relief hearing her mate's SUV driving toward their house.

Belle released a wriggling Walker and watched the boy toddle off toward the front door with his mother close behind him.

"I don't know where he gets all his energy," Melinda said. "He certainly keeps up with his father."

For the second time that day, Belle bent over in laughter because as the front door opened, Harris, who'd been the first to walk through it, found himself with a bouncing toddler at his feet, trying to climb up his legs, shouting "Da-Da" as loud as he could to get his attention. Belle swore she saw her Alpha wince when the boy extended his claws and climbed up his father's legs.

"Aww, did you miss your daddy?" Harris asked his son, whipping him up and throwing him into the air only to catch him a second later.

"Oh dear God, Harris," Melinda shouted.

"It's okay, chick. Remember, he has his dad in him." Harris beamed at his mate and then engulfed her against his huge body.

"I forget sometimes, that's all. You couldn't do that with a normal seven-month-old."

"A normal seven-month-old doesn't have claws and can't change into a cat either." Harris kissed the top of his mate's head.

"I missed you too," Melinda said, kissing him.

Belle watched the couple and went all gooey inside. The love they shared was clear to see. She noticed movement behind them and stopped still when she met the eyes of a strange male. In between Harris and Felix stood a man with clear blue eyes that were looking straight into hers.

Her heart stuttered a beat, and her breath froze in her chest. Her tiger leapt to the front of her mind and roared. It looked like fate was coming to her after all. Her mate had just walked in the door.

Chapter 4

"Belle?"

Belle's eyes flickered to Felix when he walked in front of the man, blocking her sight of him.

"Yes?" she asked. Did she miss something?

"You okay?"

"Are you going to introduce us?" She nodded toward the man with the gorgeous eyes.

"This is the newest occupant of our village. Shawn Burr, ti—"

"Tiger," she interrupted.

Already her own tiger was roaring and scraping along the inside of her skin, wanting to get to their mate. *Mate.* It hit her hard. She had a mate and he was here.

Why was he just standing there staring at her? Why was she for that matter? Shifters knew automatically who their mate was. The general pattern of meeting them was see-fuck-mate, then spend years getting to know each other. But something inside her held back. She could smell the slight tint of blood coming from him and mixed in with it was…fear? One side of his face had the mottled mix of blue and green bruising. His eyes held the tired look of 'been there, done that, don't want to do it again'.

"Hi," she said, holding out her hand. "I'm Belle."

Felix watched her with a frown on his face.

"It's okay," she said, patting her beta's arm as she walked

past, her hand still held out toward Shawn. Briefly, she wondered why Felix would look concerned, but she wanted to feel Shawn's skin on hers, to feel some kind of comfort or connection from his tiger knowing hers.

With a little hesitation Shawn lifted his hand, placed it in hers, and shook it with a slight squeeze. Warmth flowed through her, and her cat purred deep and low. She could feel the recognition from both of their tigers knowing each other. It was brief and fleeting, and when he released her hand after a few seconds, she felt the loss immediately. He moved his gaze away from her and looked over her shoulder, dismissing her.

"I know you feel it," she whispered. As soon as the words left her mouth, she felt unsure. "Tell me you do at least…please."

She was begging? Her, the big, bad enforcer female, was begging her mate to tell her she was right? A small growl left her. Shawn's body tensed and frightened eyes looked back at her. What the fuck?

"Belle, we need to talk." Harris's voice came from behind her.

"But…" She swiveled her head toward Harris then back to Shawn.

"Belle!" Her Alpha growled low. It was a sound she couldn't ignore; her Alpha wanted attention and would receive it.

Turning, she bowed her head toward Harris, her gaze firmly attached to the tiled floor. "Apologies, Alpha."

"Come into my office," he ordered her. Harris led the way

toward his office, one arm around his mate's waist and his son in his other arm.

With one last glance toward Shawn she followed.

"Felix, show our new guest his home," Harris instructed his brother.

The shelves lining the walls of Harris's office were filled with various books and an assortment of paperwork. Although the room was cleaner since he'd met Melinda, it was the one place in his house that her feminine touch hadn't reached…yet. But Belle knew it wouldn't be long before something pink or frilly found its way into the room.

Harris sat in his huge leather chair behind his desk and held a wriggling Walker on his lap. Melinda sat on a small couch near the window.

Harris kissed his boy on the head and turned his attention to Belle. "Mate?" he asked.

Belle nodded, automatically knowing he was asking about her and Shawn. She sat down in a chair opposite him. "As soon as I saw him, I knew. Are you going to tell me why we're not jumping each other's bones right now and why he is injured?"

It didn't surprise her to already feel protective over the male. She wanted to find the person who had injured him and break every single bone in their body. She hated seeing the glimpse of pain and hurt in his eyes for those few brief moments she had looked at him.

"What I tell you now goes no further than these walls, unless he speaks the words himself. I will also tell you that it will be harder for him to admit than you will think."

"I want to know who hurt him so I can find them and snap them in half," she growled.

"Belle." Harris's voice lowered a few octaves, and his eyes flashed bright blue, showing his displeasure she'd spoken out. She again ducked her head but kept her eyes on his. "He is in a world of pain right now, take it easy and slow with him. This mating for two shifters is going to be slower than normal. The person who harmed him is still out there—"

"He is safe here," she interrupted, which only again led him to show his annoyance.

After a moment's silence and her show of deference, he continued. "He has been in an abusive relationship for years."

Belle was shocked. The thought of her mate hitting a woman was completely unacceptable. Now that she knew that, even if he was her mate, she couldn't think of mating him. If he ever attempted to raise a hand toward her, he'd find himself on his arse. Was that why he was hurt? Had she fought back?

"Don't even think it," Harris warned as if he knew her thoughts. "Think, Belle. What does his attitude say? What was in his eyes? His scent?"

"Think what? He hits women and you bring him here to safety? Whoever is after him des—"

"Shut up!" Harris growled again, deep and low.

His son looked up at him, his lower lip quivered and tears welled in his eyes.

"Sorry, son," he whispered. He kissed the boy's forehead and gave him a little tickle on his belly.

Walker's mood shifted straight away. Belle sat silently, watching her Alpha turn from leader to father. Once Walker was happy again Harris turned his attention back to her.

"What was his first reaction to you, and think about it before you open your mouth."

Belle thought back. When his eyes had met hers it was shock first at seeing her, which was understandable…she had felt the same thing. Then there was nothing. He'd closed off, shut down. Until she'd held out her hand. It was fear she scented. His eyes showed pain, worry, and feelings of unworthiness?

"He was the one being abused?" she asked, unsure if that could even happen. Was this a joke? Did men get abused? How did they allow it? She knew not one of her team of enforcers would raise a hand to her or any other female in their village. Even when it came to sparring in their weekly exercises the men were reluctant to be her teammate. But to actually allow a woman to beat two shades of shit out of you on a regular basis?

"Yes. The last incident led to him being stabbed. His friend and boss managed to get him to admit it and make a statement to the police. Alas, it seems his ex-partner has disappeared, we think maybe with the help of her five brothers."

"Really? How long had he been in the relationship?" she asked, slumping back into her chair.

"Around four years."

"Fucking hell. How did he let that happen?" she asked, confused.

"What do you mean *let it happen*?" Melinda asked, sitting up on the sofa.

"Well… He's a man…how could he let himself be abused like that? He could have walked out, left her."

"What, just because he's a man he can't be the victim? Because he's a man he shouldn't have *let* this happen? I think he's a fucking strong person to go through four years of abuse, four years of being trodden on like a bag of shit, to be hurt and not raise a hand to his partner. He must have loved her deeply to stay with her after the first time it happened, and I bet if you asked him what kept him in the relationship at the end, it was shame, embarrassment, and fear, and maybe the thought that he deserved to be there."

Belle had never seen Melinda looking so angry. She sat thinking about everything her friend and alpha female had said, about everything she herself had thought. Melinda was right. If he'd been a woman, the first thought would have been to chase the bastard down and break bones. She now felt shame in judging him as she had.

"I'm so sorry," she whispered to Melinda, trying to swallow the lump in the back of her throat. "You're right. It's just hard to believe." She stood and glanced toward the office door, the need to see her mate hitting her hard and furious. "I need to go see him. I need to understand, to be there for him. I want to be there to show him not all women are bastards."

"The police had to be told where he was staying, they will need to talk to him more. If his partner—"

"Ex," Belle interrupted Harris and received a glare for it. When she dropped her head, he carried on.

"If his *ex*-partner is found, then they will want to inform him. I'm letting you know because the enforcers will have to be on guard for visiting coppers who don't know how to use the phone," Harris said sarcastically.

"Thank you, Alpha." Belle nodded and strode toward the door, eager to get to her mate.

"Just remember to take it easy, Belle," Harris warned.

She again lowered her head a fraction in respect and left the office. Before the door shut behind her Walker's giggles filled the air.

Chapter 5

After showing Shawn around the small, fully furnished one-bedroom flat Felix had left. He'd informed Shawn that Harris would come to see him in a few days, once he was fully healed and rested, to talk about work.

Shawn sat on the two-seater couch in the sitting room, feeling lost. So far he'd been treated well and shown that this new community cared about the people that joined them. The fridge was fully stocked as well as the freezer, and he had clothes hanging up in his new wardrobe, but the sense of loss seemed to hit him the hardest. He supposed he was still in shock. But looking around, nothing was his; the last four years of his life had been washed away so to speak.

Harris and Felix had offered to take him back to his house to pack up his clothes, but the thought of going back to the place had his heart thundering in his chest and cold sweats breaking out over his body. Harris had even offered to send someone else to do the deed once he was settled in Stonesdale, but again Shawn refused his offer. Rosie micromanaged everything, even down to his clothes. If he was to start again, he would do it his way.

On the trip to the village Harris had filled him in on all the rules and regulations that the community kept to. "Normally, anyone who wishes to join our community has been thoroughly vetted and informed of the rules then given a few days to either accept or decline. Alas, in your circumstance we are doing this now. But you aren't the first we have invited to join us immediately. One part of your case, the vetting, was done before I met you. You will be safe here. We have enforcers that constantly prowl around the village, keeping a look out for unwanted visitors. Hopefully, you'll be able to restart your life in a better circumstance. I am only sorry to see you lose everything in the process, but yet again, you aren't the first."

Shawn hoped his new Alpha's words were true. But he knew it was going to be a bitch to try to put the last few years behind him and move forward. Over the last few days he had accepted the fact that he'd been in an abusive relationship, which was easier than admitting it to others. He kept a mantra going in his head when he felt most lost and down. *What doesn't kill you, only makes you stronger.*

Even feeling as rotten as he did, when they'd entered the Alpha's small, quaint cottage Shawn couldn't help but smile when the Alpha's kit had climbed his father's leg, eager to see him, shouting out "Da-Da". However, the smile had quickly faded when he saw the most beautiful pair of lavender eyes he'd ever seen in his life. She had a thin layer of mascara on and what looked like a thin, black line of pencil on her bottom lid, but otherwise she was all natural. He hated the taste of lipstick anyway. Shock had torn through him as he stared at the stunning female…his mate? His tiger roared to life inside of him and stretched against his skin. His cock engorged with blood as he inhaled deeply to scent her. Honey and wild daisies, mixed in with a tigress.

Mate, go to her, grab her, fuck her, mate her, forget other horrible female, his tiger had urged.

For a split second he'd been close to taking a step toward her. He'd wanted to scoop her up into his arms, carry her off to the nearest bed, and fuck her stupid. His injuries were forgotten, and the years of abuse he'd suffered dusted and blew away while he looked into those eyes. But then in a flash the memories of the last few years came rushing back to him. Everything suddenly weighed him down when she offered her hand in greeting and introduced herself.

He placed his hand into her small one and felt the warmth and love come from both of their tigers. He knew they both saw each other as mates. But instead of acknowledging it, he pulled his hand back and shifted his gaze away from hers.

His tiger had roared in disagreement and sorrow, insisting that they needed her, that she could help them mend. But it was too soon. As much as he wanted to talk to Belle the thought of telling her about his life made him sick. It wasn't the thought of Rosie that held him back; his love for her had slowly dwindled with each passing day. No, it was the fear of rejection, the fear of what she might think of him when she found out what had happened.

As he had watched Belle walk away from him, following his new Alpha into his office, Felix had offered to show him around the home they were going to rent him. And now here he was in a one-bedroom flat with the chance of a new life and his mate just down the road. Just the thought of her made him feel a little stronger. He knew she was the one he was meant to be with. He had a lot of *what if's.* But if he chose to live his life in *what if's* he knew he wouldn't get anywhere. He'd done that for years now. *Perhaps she will give me time to adjust.*

A knock at his door brought him out of his turmoil of thoughts. Inhaling, he smelled wild daisies and honey and knew Belle was on the other side.

You can do this. We are together now. Shawn felt an overwhelming flow of warmth and love coming from his beast. He was glad his tiger was once again a part of him.

Opening the door, Shawn's cock grew instantly stiff and uncomfortable in his jeans. As they stood staring at each other he could scent her arousal. He could imagine her wet and ready for him. They weren't far from a bedroom…he could take her, fill her, and make her theirs. A sense of peace rippled through him, before his world crashed again with *what if's.*

"I just passed Felix, and he mentioned you haven't been on a run in a while. Want to join me?"

Shawn nodded before thinking. It might help him heal a little bit quicker as well as relax some. Letting his tiger meets hers could be the ice-breaker he needed.

"Sounds good," he said, feeling a little more positive. "Want to change here?"

An almost seductive smile lit up Belle's face. The image of her underneath him, panting and begging him to fuck her harder, had his dick pressing against his zipper.

"Sure."

He stepped back from the doorway, moved around the sofa in the living area, and began stripping. Even living with a human for four years hadn't stripped him of feeling comfortable in his own skin. He knew he had a good body, six-pack, muscles, etcetera. Shifters tended not to worry about being naked around each other. It was one thing Rosie had hated about him though; she always made sure he kept his shirt on, especially when he was outside. Being outside bare-chested was absolutely forbidden.

Carefully, Shawn peeled away the tape that held a pad of gauze over his stomach wound. Looking down at it, he saw it still had a little way to go before completely healing. A long, thin line of skin held together by black stitches was red and raised. Give it a shift or two, and by tomorrow or the next day his skin wouldn't even show he'd had a wound there. He made a mental note to see the village doctor tomorrow to have the stitches removed. He unwrapped the bandages on his arms. They too were still red, but with fresh skin instead of the blistered mess they'd been a few days ago.

He could hear the rustling of clothes behind him. The temptation to turn around was too much, so he swiveled slowly, catching Belle fully nude before she began her shift. She had a perfect pair of tits with a perky set of nipples on them. Her pussy was well-groomed with a thin strip of hair down the middle. Her figure looked like an old cola bottle. She had wide hips that tapered into a narrow waist. *Just over five and a half feet of soft, succulent heaven*, he thought.

He watched white and black fur slip from her pores and

cover her skin while bones cracked, and in a few seconds a wonderful white Siberian tiger stood before him, purring, calling with a chuff to his tiger.

Shawn quickly began his shift to cover his raging hard-on. His Siberian tiger was orange with black stripes. Shawn watched through his tiger's eyes as the pair greeted each other, rubbing against each other in a loving manner. Both cats purred deep and low. Each tiger in turn rubbed their scent glands on the top of the other's head, making sure anyone who came across them knew the pair were mates.

It was Belle's cat who made the first move. She turned around, showing off her backside, and tucked her tail down the side of her body, then she lowered her forepaws down and threw her arse in the air. Shawn could feel his tiger's heat, his willingness to mount the female. But before he could take a step forward, Belle's tiger took off, running through the door and outside.

She's a tease. His tiger growled and purred, sounding like a motor. *I like it.*

He ran after his mate. Over rocks and grass, through mud and past the cracks in the earth, the tigers ran chasing each other. They head-butted and scuffled, enjoying each other's company. Shawn left his tiger to reign and enjoyed the freedom of it.

After taking a while, but with a show of dominance, Shawn's tiger caught up to his mate, and with his teeth firmly encased around the nape of her neck, his tiger mounted the teasing female. Shawn felt everything—the moment his tiger's cock filled his mate, each and every stroke, and then the explosion of both animal's orgasms.

Once the male had pulled out from the female, she rolled over several times, purring in delight. Satisfaction seemed to shine from her. Shawn's beast relaxed and lay next to the female, licking around his mate's neck. Images of Belle lying next to him, naked and dripping with his seed, filled Shawn's mind. His tiger certainly agreed with that too. Curling around each other, the tigers' colors mixing together, both of the cats napped.

"It would seem both our tigers are happy with each other." Belle's voice filled his head. It had been years since he'd heard another shifter's voice in his mind. It felt both weird and comforting.

"Yes, it does. He is extremely happy right now. It's a shame to disturb them," he replied.

"We don't have to, we can just talk, learn a little about each other."

Get to know his new mate? With both their tigers sleeping, he knew he had some time on his hands. Accepting he was safe enough behind his beast, he metaphorically shrugged his shoulders and opened his mind.

"A captive audience?" he asked jokingly.

"You could say that." She chuckled.

After a few minutes of silence, he spoke up. *"I can imagine our Alpha has told you about me."* Shawn wondered exactly what Harris had said to Belle.

"He told me that you were in an abusive relationship, and she is still out there, probably being protected by her brothers." She

paused.

He sensed the guilt coming from her and waited.

"*I have a confession to make. When Harris told me what had happened. I didn't understand, and I had thoughts that...well, that I'm ashamed of. I cannot apologize enough for that, and I hope you can forgive me.*"

Shawn had an image of Belle on her knees with her head bent. His automatic reaction was to soothe her. "*You don't have to apologize. I have no idea what your reaction actually was, although I can imagine. If you assumed it was me who did the abusing, I've learned that's the normal reaction—*"

"*Please let me finish. You will understand then.*" After a moment's pause Belle carried on. "*When Harris said you had been in an abusive relationship, yes, I automatically thought it was you who was the abusive party. I know I didn't have to tell you this, you would never have known, but I would have known. Will you tell me what happened one day? I want to be there for you, to let you know that not all women are like that. You are my mate, Shawn, and I want us to be happy, I want you to be happy.*"

He could feel the truth in her words. Their tigers were extremely happy and had now mated as far as they were concerned. There was no escape from the upcoming relationship with Belle, he knew that. But it wasn't the feeling of dread and being trapped into being with Belle. He felt unsure, which was normal he supposed. The thought of separating the two beasts was inconceivable. Even after the way Rosie had treated him, he had loved her, and for some unknown reason he still felt affection for her, or maybe it was lingering affection of how things had been at one time. He was so confused he couldn't be sure. But deep down in his heart he knew if Belle was meant to be his, she would wait.

"I have felt so alone for so long now... I need time..."

"I can give you that. But know you're not alone now."

Chapter 6

With Shawn quiet and lost in his own thoughts, Belle allowed her mind to go over everything that had happened in the short time since she'd met him. As far as her tiger was concerned, it was now mated for life. So far she knew very little about Shawn; only that he had been hurt, he'd spent four years in an abusive relationship, and he was her mate. She wondered how long it would take the man to allow her fully into his life. She couldn't wait to go home tonight and tell her parents she had found her mate. Surely they would have some advice for her.

An idea flashed—if her tiger now thought of itself as mated, then maybe that would give Belle a way to get closer to Shawn. She guessed it was going to take him a while to be comfortable, let alone to fully accept her. She made a plan…daily runs with their tigers. Hopefully, she could get Shawn to agree to allow his tiger to play with hers each day.

The tigers strolled together after waking from their nap, taking a casual stroll back home. Now and then one of the beasts would purposely rub up against the other or stroke its head along the other's body. To Belle they seemed so in tune with each other, and she hoped one day that she and Shawn would have that.

"*Shawn?*" she asked tentatively, unsure if he was still locked inside his own mind and would answer.

"*I'm here,*" he responded.

"*I guess Harris is going to give you a few days to settle in before talking about work?"*

"Yeah, but I'm not sure where he will be able to put me that I can be productive. I'm not one of those men that can put their hands to anything. I like people, that's why I chose to be a receptionist. But I'll try anything."

"Harris is good at reading people. I bet you a pound to a penny that he will offer you the perfect position for you."

"You're an enforcer, right?" Shawn asked.

"Yep," she said with pride. *"The lone female on a team of dominant males. When I first joined I had to put up with months of ribbing and practical jokes. Oh, and then there were the sexual innuendos."* She sighed. *"But during a training session I got lucky, I managed to put both Harris and Felix on their tails. The men were awed enough that I get respect now. I also have quite a bit of respect from both the Alpha and beta now. If anyone gives me shit over being a female, they get extra training or shifts. In fact, I could say my best friend is Felix."* Belle mentally smiled. Her tiger passed a stream of energy, both pride and passion to her.

"Have you ever...slept with him?"

Belle couldn't help but smile. *"Is that a hint of jealousy?"*

"Um... I... Well... I don't know you that well yet."

"No, but you know I'm your mate," she stated, trying to get her man to admit to his emotion.

"Yes... Okay, yes, I feel a little jealous."

Belle smiled again. Maybe there was hope for them yet. *"The answer is no. I have slept with no one. I wanted to be able to give my true mate something of me that I've given to no other."* Belle waited for Shawn to fully take in what she just said. Mentally, she could have heard a pin drop in the stunned silence.

"But what if you had never met him...me?"

"I suppose that eventually, before my beast became too despondent, I would have imprinted on someone. But for now I had hope, and thankfully fate seems to have a plan for you and I."

Belle felt disappointed to see they were near Shawn's new home. At his door his tiger nudged her in first. After they shifted and re-dressed they stood staring at each other in an awkward silence until she spoke.

"Want me to re-dress your wounds before I go?" She motioned toward his torso and arms.

"No, I was actually thinking about seeing the doc and getting the stitches taken out tomorrow. As for my arms, another shift and I'll be fully healed."

Belle examined his handsome face. "The bruises on your face have all but disappeared now."

She smiled at him. His eyes had a little more sparkle in them since his shift, but she held her tongue with that information. He dropped his gaze and looked toward the floor, a slight blush on his cheeks.

"I'll be going," she said, taking a step backward toward the door. If she hadn't been staring at his face, she would have missed the brief emotion of sorrow that flickered over it. Would he want her to stay?

"I'm sorry," he said.

"Sorry?"

"Yeah, I know this isn't the conventional way shifters would go about—"

Stepping forward, Belle interrupted him. "Conventional?" She snorted. "We live in a village filled with a variety of feline shifters, some of which, usually, wouldn't be caught dead with the other. There is nothing *normal* about that." She air quoted the word *normal*. "The majority of people in this place have had their own shit to deal with at some point, just like you. There are also those who have always lived here in peace and harmony, like me. We cohabitate well. Sure, we have problems at times, but we work them out. I am going to ask you to do one thing for me," she said before stepping back again. She had to leave, because his scent was driving her wild.

She wanted to rake her hands down his naked skin. To feel his body close to hers. But his eyes stopped her; they were filled with so much sorrow that she wanted to wrap her arms around him and never let him go. She wanted to tell him that with her beside him, no one would ever hurt him again.

"If I can, I will." He lifted his gaze up to look at her.

"From now on, say *sorry* only when you've done something wrong. Not because you feel like you have to."

He stared at her with an expression of total confusion.

"Living in this community that offers sanctuary to those in need, I've come across a few shifters that have been abused. Some of them, when they first moved here, felt they even had to apologize for living. It had been drummed into them. I want you to know I'm glad you're here, alive and safe amongst us. This may not be the normal way to meet a mate, but then what is?"

Glancing down at his mouth, she saw his lips move as if to form an automatic *sorry*. She looked back up into his eyes, raising her eyebrow, and he paused with the tiniest of smiles appearing instead of the continued word. She wanted to take the few steps toward him and place a kiss on his cheek, but she was unsure if she should. So instead she turned toward the door and stepped outside.

"Want to do this tomorrow?" she asked before closing his door. "Me, you, our tigers?"

His face flickered with an array of emotions then finally settled with what she thought might be acceptance. "Sure, why not? My beast enjoyed today immensely, and if I were to be honest, I enjoyed the freedom of being with my beast again." A bigger smile appeared on his face. "He also just threatened that if I said no, he wouldn't talk to me again," he admitted with a visible shiver and a wrinkled nose. "Been there, done that. Wouldn't want to go there again." Shawn swallowed, and she watched his Adam's apple bob up and down. "He's still angry at me, but is learning to accept what *I put myself through*." The last few words were added in a sarcastic manner as if he didn't agree with his tiger. "Plus, I enjoyed being in your company today. Thank you."

"You don't see the abuse you went through as he…and others do." Again, she wanted to go to him and wrap her arms around him, just to let him know all relationships weren't like the one he'd experienced.

"It wasn't always that bad…" He let the sentence trail off.

"Well, it's time to heal and start anew. I'm glad you here, no matter the circumstances. Goodnight, Shawn. See you tomorrow." Belle blew him a kiss, and then pulled the door closed.

She didn't know how long she stood outside his closed door before finally forcing herself to walk away. She needed a hug from her mother.

* * * *

Mate! Shawn repeated the word over and over in his mind. *Mate!*

Our mate! One who won't hurt you. Shawn's tiger purred, sending him images of his earlier mating.

How do we know that? Rosie didn't hurt in the beginning.

I know! his tiger argued, getting a little pissed. *My mate, she tell me her human is good woman. She was asked to be beta today while Felix is away.*

Shawn suddenly felt sick to the very depths of his stomach. Belle had been offered a management position? It was like history repeating itself. Rosie's mood had taken a turn for the worse when she became manager at the hotel.

She may be sweet and innocent now, but power changes people, he told his tiger and sent images to him of Rosie before and after her promotion.

No, his tiger snapped at him, growling. *Rosie was a bitch before and after. Do not cancel tomorrow… Please.*

Shawn slumped onto the couch, lost in an array of memories and emotions. The glee he felt meeting his mate, the guilt he felt for leaving Rosie. It was all tying him up in knots. Eventually, it was the shadows filling his home that brought him out of his stupor.

Standing, he placed one of the ready-made meals from the fridge into the microwave and warmed it up. After eating, he climbed into the shower. The warm water raining down helped him relax, and his tiger decided to play a few mind tricks of his own. He sent Shawn images of the afternoon mating with his mate.

Okay, okay. He sighed. *You win. I won't cancel tomorrow. You're a horny beast.*

His tiger purred deep inside him. *If you let your mate into heart, then you will be horny too.*

Shawn shook his head. How long had it been since he'd had sex? Rosie had turned cold and frigid when it came to sex. She hadn't let him touch her in over six months. What would it feel like to be inside Belle? The warmth of her skin, the tightness of her pussy. His hands skimming over her lush curves, caressing her tits that would overflow in his palms.

Blood rushed south and filled his cock. He couldn't help but groan. He placed his fingers around his hard shaft and closed his eyes. He tightened his hold to the way he liked it and began stroking gently up and down.

Placing his free hand on the wall of the shower, he leaned against it and widened his stance. His thumb rubbed along the top of the mushroomed head and spread the pre-cum that had leaked from the slit. He wished he had the guts to go find his mate and take her like a normal shifter would do, to fuck her until they both forgot their names.

As he thought about her incredible boobs and the fine line of fur he'd seen between her legs, his strokes became faster. He imagined her lower lips glistening with her arousal. The look on her face as he brought her to completion. He cried out, her name on his lips. He opened his eyes to see his cum spurt from his cock in stringy threads to fall to the floor and wash down the drain with the water. When his breathing slowed, he turned off the water and dried himself.

He walked around the house checking the windows and doors, and making sure everything was neat and tidy as he always did. Rosie would scream bloody murder if a single item was out of place. Reaching his room, he climbed into the king-sized bed. He couldn't help himself, he spread out wide on the bed, pulling the covers up to his waist. No Rosie to moan he was taking all the covers or taking up too much space. She'd never been one to spoon or touch in bed apart from the random requests for sex.

A tiny sliver of a smile lifted his lips when he realized Rosie wouldn't ever scream at him again. He curled up and drifted off to sleep thinking of Belle.

Chapter 7

Three days later, Shawn was walking through Stonesdale with Harris. He had spent the last few days healing and investigating the small community. It was quite a friendly place. People often stopped and spoke to him, welcoming him to the village. Now that he was fully healed and settled in, he was more than ready to work again.

Belle had come by every day, both of them giving their tigers full rein and letting them roam. It was coming to the end of April, and their beasts loved to sit and watch the new spring babies frolic with their mothers. Shawn drew on the calming emotions his tiger gained from doing that. He found it easier to be around Belle, and they began sharing stories from their past. The antics they managed to get up to as kids. He even caught himself opening up and telling her about his parents. He wished they had found this place or somewhere like it. If they had, they might still be alive.

Shawn followed Harris into the village doctor's surgery. Shawn had just been here yesterday to have his stitches removed. It was the elderly lion shifter who greeted the Alpha.

"Ben." Harris shook the man's hand. "This is the gentleman I was telling you about." He gestured toward Shawn.

"Aye." Ben nodded with a genuine smile on his face. "We've met before."

"Good hands, sir." Shawn smiled at Ben.

"Not as sturdy as they used to be, but they still have life in them yet. It looks like you came along at the right time, young man. My last receptionist just had twins and she decided to become a full-time mother, which leaves an open space. You up for it?" Ben asked.

"What, just start?" Shawn asked, surprised. "No interview or anything?"

"You have the Alpha's recommendation, boy. I trust him. He told me you were a receptionist before at a lawyer's office. If you could deal with the paperwork that job entails, you can deal with it here."

Shawn took the old man's offered hand again and shook it. "Thank you, sir. I will make you proud, and the Alpha, of course." He turned to Harris with a thankful smile.

"Leaving you two to it," Harris said to the pair of them. "Shawn, come by to see me later, and we'll talk about the rent, etcetera." Without waiting for an answer, Harris walked out of the surgery, giving a wave of his hand as he left.

Turning back to the doc, Shawn began his first work day in the Stonesdale doctor's surgery.

* * * *

"Hey there, handsome."

Shawn lifted his head to look at the clock then Belle. He had been so engrossed in his work he hadn't heard her come into the building. It was late afternoon, time to go home soon. Shawn was looking forward to a run with Belle.

"Hey." He smiled.

His tiger purred deep inside him, and Shawn could feel the

hope flowing from him. *Time for an evening stroll,* he told his beast and received a flow of love from him.

"Ready for our run?" he asked Belle, standing up from the small reception desk.

"Oh bugger, that's why I came. Felix is leaving in a few days, so I have to go over to his place later for a few more 'lessons' to keep things straight." The smile on her face didn't reach her eyes.

Shawn's heart stuttered a beat with the misery he felt. He had actually been looking forward to tonight. "Um, okay, no problem. Maybe tomorrow?"

"How about tomorrow morning before work?" she asked with a sparkle in her eyes. "I really am sorry about tonight, babe, but once Felix buggers off I'll have more free time. Promise."

His instant thought was a sarcastic *yeah, okay, sure. Let me down slowly just like Rosie did.* But he pushed it back into the 'negative thoughts because of *her*' box.

"Sure, tomorrow morning." He nodded, plastering a fake smile on his face.

Belle had slowly but surely managed to creep her way into his heart. He'd been there nearly a week now and already his thoughts about Belle and her luscious curves were becoming more prominent than his thoughts about Rosie. He'd started sorting out his emotions bit by bit, putting the ones he had for Rosie into a box in his mind and sitting on it. He was still afraid they would jump back out at him and his Belle might not be able to climb over the wall they would create. *His Belle.*

Watching Belle walk back out the door he felt her loss more severely than he had felt leaving Rosie. He knew he shouldn't compare the two women, but it was so hard. All he had ever known was Rosie, she had been his woman for so long. At one point he had been ready to imprint on her rather than wait for his true mate— Belle. Shawn shook his head at the thought. He knew he had to concentrate on Belle now.

Gathering the papers he'd been sorting, he shuffled them until they were neat then turned to grab his light summer jacket and popped his head inside Ben's office to say goodnight.

* * * *

Belle had seen the hurt in Shawn's eyes and the fake smile on his face and knew she was getting to him. She felt some satisfaction because for the first time since they met she had smelled a tinge of lust coming off him mixed in with all his manly scent. But she didn't like the hurt she had caused him at cancelling their plans. It was Felix's fault, and she would make him suffer tonight.

"Belle, we have incoming. Large black SUV. North." Felix's voice filled her mind.

Immediately, she went on alert. *"I was already heading to the Alpha's house to meet you, but moving faster now,"* she replied, and started running toward her destination.

She inwardly smiled, knowing she'd just told Felix she had been taking her time getting to their meeting. She knew too that she would have been one of the first to be told about any visitors being she was on the Alpha's mate protection duty. Harris loved the village, but he loved his mate and child just a tiny bit more; in his eyes they always came first. Each of the enforcers on patrol would now be on the alert, either in their human or their cat form.

Even with the village being out in the sticks, they would often get visitors. But because of the community being shifters and some of their occupants running from other shifters, the visitors were watched very carefully. Harris kept a tight ship when it came to the people he protected.

Just as Belle reached the driveway of Harris's house, she heard the vehicle. As it drove past her, toward the center of the village, she watched it, taking in every single detail she could.

"Black SUV heading toward the center of town. Tinted windows, but I made out two suited male occupants in the front and one unknown in the back. I'll relay the number plate to Larry."

"Aye aye," Felix replied.

Felix's *yes* was often *aye aye*. She'd told him once he sounded like a fucking pirate. She'd even called him 'Captain Pussy Cat' once. The bastard had repaid her for that comment by assigning her a few extra shifts.

With her senses on full alert, Belle ran up to the house and walked inside. She found both Melinda and Walker in the kitchen.

"Hey there, little man," she cooed at Walker, ignoring Melinda's questioning look. "Whatcha got there, mate?" she said, looking into a small bowl containing his food. "Mmm, looks like spaghetti. Yummy." She moaned, making the boy smile.

She could feel Melinda's eyes boring into her.

"Are you going to keep ignoring me?" Melinda asked.

Belle sighed, but turned to her friend with a small smile.

"Harris told me to stay in the house, then rushed out of it like a bat out of hell. What's going on?" Melinda asked.

"We have a visitor, that's all." Belle shrugged.

"What kind?"

"Not sure yet, just a black SUV with three occupants. Not the normal visitor type if you get my meaning."

"You mean the ones in the scruffy four-wheelers or the tourists that wear hiking boots and look like they're ready for whatever weather is thrown at them." Melinda chuckled. It was only last week that they'd had a small group of hikers come through the village wearing clothes from raincoats to shorts, topped off with huge clodhopper boots on their feet.

"Yep."

"You think it could be anything serious?" Melinda's face changed to one of worry. It hadn't been that long ago since her own troubles brought her to Stonesdale.

"Not sure yet, just waiting for a top up of info," Belle said, tapping her temple. "I'm about to take a wander."

After planting a kiss on Walker's head, Belle slowly wandered around the Alpha's house, using all of her senses to make sure that all was well there. But instead of feeling calm as she usually did, she felt anxious. Ever since she'd been told of the vehicle she'd wanted to make sure Shawn was okay, but first she had to make sure Melinda and her son were safe.

"Shawn?" she asked, reaching out to his mind. Nothing. She waited a few seconds then tried again. *"Shawn?"*

"I'm with Harris and three policemen. I'll talk to you in a bit," he answered, his voice strained.

Worry flooded her. Why were the police with him? They must have been the ones in the car. For the first time since being an enforcer, she felt torn. She wanted to be with her mate, to be at his side.

"Felix?" She quickly tuned into the beta's mind.

"Is it important?"

"It's about the three coppers."

"How do you know about the visitors?" Felix asked.

"Shawn told me."

"Let us deal with this, Belle."

"But—"

"Not now." A growled warning was thrown back.

"But that's my mate,"

"Belle, not now!" Felix answered with a growl that resonated around in her head.

What was she to do? Abandon her post, give up everything she had worked so hard to obtain? She wanted to howl. She also knew she had to trust her Alpha and beta to be there for her mate.

A growl slipped from between her lips as she walked inside the Alpha's house. She received a surprised then worried look from Melinda. She couldn't help but frown back at the woman. "It's nothing, just me being pissed off," she groaned.

Melinda chuckled. "I bet that has to do with a man."

"Of course." Belle sighed. It was going to be a long evening.

* * * *

Shawn had just walked out of the surgery when a black SUV pulled up outside the small police station next to it. Three well-groomed, suited men climbed out of the vehicle. The way they carried themselves automatically shouted *law enforcement*.

A shiver went through Shawn. Something deep inside him said these men were there because of him. Should he go home and wait, or simply enter the police station and say...say what? *Hi? Are you here for me?*

Shawn realized his mind-set had yet again slipped into the past. He felt guilty, unsure. He wondered what he'd done wrong. Shawn couldn't make his feet move to walk anywhere. He kept trying to tell himself that these men weren't there for him, he hadn't done anything wrong. He stood frozen in place, his mind in turmoil, both negative and positive thoughts trading blows.

It was Harris and Felix who brought him out of his mental unrest. Felix placed a hand on his shoulder and gave him a worried look, while Harris walked straight into the police station. Shawn breathed in a large lungful of air and released it. His skin was clammy and having Felix look at him with worried eyes wasn't helping him stand tall and proud like he thought he should be.

"Panic moment?" Felix asked.

"They are here for me, right?" Shawn asked Felix, already knowing the answer. He received a small nod in acknowledgement.

"Harris just informed me," Felix said, tapping his temple.

"Okay, let's get this over with." Shawn sighed and walked into the police station with Felix beside him.

Chapter 8

"Ah, just the man we wanted to see." The village copper, a portly lion shifter known as Garrett greeted him as he walked into the building's reception area.

With the three suited coppers along with Harris and Garrett standing in the small room, it felt claustrophobic. The feeling was intensified by the fact that every single pair of eyes in the room was staring at him.

"This is Detective Johnathon Canker, Detective Harry Small, and Detective Louis Frank." Garrett pointed to each man as he introduced them. "They're here to question you about Miss Rosie O'Hare."

All three men were tall, clean-shaven, and their suit jackets didn't have a single crease in them. It briefly crossed Shawn's mind that for them to still be perfect after sitting in a car for an hour or more they must have taken them off. It was plain to see Garrett was trying to control the situation in his office. By making the introductions he was making sure the visiting detectives knew this was his police station no matter what their rank.

Johnathon Canker stared over Shawn's shoulder to look at Felix. "You are?" he questioned, short and sharp.

Shawn looked behind him to see Felix's lips lift in a smirk, his eyes filling with defiant mirth. "Leaving," he simply stated before striding out of the building.

Ballzee, Shawn's tiger said.

He is off on some kind of travels soon. I get the impression he doesn't like this kind of authority.

After a brief moment of silence one of the detectives spoke. "Interrogation room?"

Shawn felt dread seep through him. Interrogation room? When had being stabbed suddenly turn into a crime?

"I'm sure we can do this in Garrett's office." Harris's deep voice, tinged with a growl, resonated through the room.

"I understand that you are the mayor here, sir, but this is police business. We're here to question Mr. Burr."

"Every single person in this community is under my care. His welfare has everything to do with me. If Mr. Burr wishes for me to leave, I will, but a solicitor will be taking my place. Otherwise, I will stay."

All eyes again turned toward Shawn. He was sure he looked nervous as hell, he certainly felt it. It wasn't because of Harris though. Having his Alpha there was quietly comforting.

Lifting his head in a defiant way, he said, "I wish for Mr. Rockwell to stay, please."

Each one of the detectives' faces seemed to pinch into annoyance, as if having a civilian in the room was going to hinder them.

"Shall we take this to my office then?" Garrett asked, breaking the suddenly intense atmosphere.

The detective who seemed to be in charge, Johnathon Canker, motioned for Garrett to lead the way.

"I'm here, Shawn, just listen to what they have to say, but if I tell you not to answer, please follow my instructions." Harris walked behind Shawn down the tight hallway. The urge to turn just to see the man's face, to look into his Alpha's eyes for both reassurance and comfort, was overwhelming. *"Head up, mate, you haven't done anything wrong."*

With just a few words Shawn heard what he needed to hear—someone believed him. His Alpha was right behind him, and he wasn't going to desert him.

Once everyone was settled in Garrett's office, which was slightly bigger than the reception room, silence crept in. Harris was standing, leaning against the wall near the door, with his arms crossed over his chest. The two detectives who had yet to speak sat in chairs beside Shawn, while the other stood stiff as a post at the side of Garrett's desk, his eyes staring firmly at Shawn. Garrett sat behind his desk, looking like the lord of the jungle.

"For three of you, and being detectives, to come this far out to question Mr. Burr, I would guess that Miss O'Hare has been found," Garrett said, leaning forward on his desk.

Detective Johnathon Canker looked toward Shawn with disgust on his face. "Miss O'Hare walked into an accident-and-emergency last night. Her condition was serious. She had several broken bones and numerous week-old bruises. She informed the medical staff her fiancé had beaten her up a week previously but she'd refused to seek medical attention because she was frightened she would be found by him. By *you*. But she couldn't withstand the pain any longer so she had to seek help. She was even worried about contacting her brothers. She was afraid they would go after you and break you in half… Her words." The detective placed his hands on Garrett's desk, leaning toward Shawn in a menacing manner. "After she allowed the medical staff to call us, she reluctantly gave a statement. She said on the night you were stabbed, she injured you in self-defense."

Shawn felt like he was going to pass out. His whole body seemed to shake in shock. Rosie was accusing him of beating her up? Claiming that she'd stabbed him because he'd hit her? Oh God! He would never raise a hand to a woman. His mother would be turning in her grave right now at the accusation. She had drummed it into him as a boy that a female should never have to cower under a man's hand. That men were stronger and should never ever raise a finger to a woman no matter what she did.

In shock, he watched as one of the detectives pulled a few sheets of paper with handwritten writing on it out of a briefcase and handed them to Johnathon.

He sat in a seat beside his fellow officers, glancing over the papers in his hand. "This is her statement, and I have read yours. I can tell you they certainly do not match. I also have a statement from your boss, Paul Hardy, as well as Rosie O'Hare's five brothers, and medical staff reports too. The evidence is pretty damming for you, Mr. Burr."

Shawn's world suddenly felt so much smaller. Damming? He wished he could talk to someone; to get reassurance this wasn't a dream. The evidence was against him? For four years he had put up with Rosie shouting and screaming at him, hitting him. She had been the one who had abused him.

Shawn sighed with reservation. So this was how it was going to go? He—the male, the supposed strong one—was automatically being put in the abuser role. Shawn wondered who the hell had battered Rosie for her to have the injuries she did. Had her brothers beaten on her? Were they trying to push the blame on him to keep her from prison? At the moment they were sure winning that race.

"So, would you like to go over your statement again, Mr. Burr? Maybe rectify a few things?"

Shawn glanced at Harris.

"*Just answer truthfully, mate. Everything will work out in the end.*"

"*I hope so.*" Shawn hoped with all his heart that he could believe Harris and things would work out for the better. For shifters it was easy to know if someone was lying or not by their scent, which came in handy, but for non-shifters, like these officers, they had to work with what they had.

"*Shawn?*" The sweet voice of his mate filled his mind.

Just the simple sound of her voice helped the bubbling anger inside of him seep away. But then sadness crept in, knowing it wasn't the time to become distracted and talk to her.

"*Shawn?*" she asked again, her voice carrying more worry in it.

"*I'm with Harris and three policemen. I'll talk to you in a bit.*" He inwardly winced. Even in his own head, his voice had sounded entirely too harsh. He'd apologize later.

Bringing his attention back to the room, he had to think who had spoken and what they'd said. Johnathon… Statement…

"Everything I said in my statement is true. I came home late from work. When I pulled up and parked Rosie was already at the front door, waiting for me. She was in a dark mood and started at me before I even entered the house—"

"What do you mean *started at you*?" Johnathon interrupted Shawn.

"She started going on about how I was just a receptionist and only had a nine-to-five job, and there was no reason for me to be late. The night before she was upset about something else, only that ended in me needing stitches."

"Stitches?" Johnathon asked.

"Yes, she threw a Buddha statue at me."

"Karma?" Johnathon chuckled evilly.

Bastard, Shawn's tiger grumbled.

"What about slipping on the wet floor that she'd just mopped?" the copper asked.

Shawn frowned, wondering what the man was talking about. The thought of Rosie washing anything, let alone mopping the floor, nearly made him laugh out loud. During all the time he'd lived with Rosie, she hadn't once cleaned any floor. Was that what Rosie had told them about how he'd sliced open his head?

"Rosie didn't mop a floor in the entire time we were together, so I have no idea what you're talking about," he answered truthfully.

"Were you having an affair, Mr. Burr?" Johnathon asked, changing the subject of the questioning.

Shawn frowned again, wondering where that question had come from. Was he pulling this stuff out of mid-air?

"I… That's not something I would do. The answer to your question is no, never!"

"So why were you late then? If you are only a receptionist…" The detective let his question trail off.

Shawn felt his cheeks heat. "I was working late. Paul had a big meeting the following day and needed some paperwork finished. I wasn't just the average receptionist, I covered as a PA too."

"Okay, so you arrived home late…"

"I made dinner while Rosie went off and did her stuff, and just as I was about to dish it up she came back into the kitchen. She was annoyed, ranting about some male that had pissed her off at work, and she threw a glass across the room. When she got like that I knew it was time to keep quiet, put my head down, and not move or utter a word. I placed the tongs I had in my hand on the counter and prayed they didn't move or make a sound."

"Miss O'Hare said you threw the glass at her when she came in and interrupted you."

"Me? Throw a glass at Rosie?" A snort escaped before Shawn could stop it. "If you knew Rosie… There was no way in hell that I would do anything like that. Not to just Rosie, but to any woman. My life would be a living hell if I even raised my voice at

Rosie…" Taking a deep breath, Shawn shook his head. "My life was a living hell anyway."

Looking up, Shawn met the copper's gaze. He couldn't help the tears that burned behind his eyes. They spilled over and began falling down his cheeks.

"I wouldn't touch her," Shawn said. "I couldn't raise a hand to her. My mother brought me up well. The thought of a man harming a woman makes me sick to my stomach."

He knew he was babbling. Embarrassment heated his cheeks as a few more tears fell down his face. He was supposed to be the man, the strong one. But there he was babbling in a room with five other men. As the tears continued to fall so did any sort of affection he might have still had for Rosie, as well as any kind of confidence and self-respect for himself. He bent his head and covered his face with his hands, ashamed he'd broken down. Everything seemed to weigh heavily on top of him. The air even seemed thinner.

"I think we need five minutes." Harris's gruff voice broke through the room's sudden silence.

"No shit!" one of the coppers cursed, his voice full of disdain.

All three policemen rose and walked from the room as Garrett followed closely behind them. Even with the door closed Shawn could hear the mutterings between them all.

"It's all an act, right?" one of the detectives said.

"I'm not so sure. We'll have to wait to see what he says when we go back in."

"Oh, fuck off. You cannot be serious. There is no way that young woman we saw with all those bruises and shit could have handed down all the abuse that *he* says she did." It was Johnathon who virtually screamed that across the room.

"There are such things as female abusers. The percentage is actually pretty high."

"No. No fucking way."

"Excuse me, gentlemen, but I actually think the young man is telling the truth." Garrett's voice broke through the officers' conversation.

"Yeah, and what makes you think that?"

"Well, besides believing the man, I also read through your file and saw the medical files as well as the…"

Shawn let his head drop and closed his eyes. He didn't want to hear any more. There was no way on earth he would raise a hand to Rosie, but if she was now in a hospital beaten to a pulp, who would believe him? Well, he knew the shifters would, because they had the ability to scent a lie. That wouldn't hold up in court though. Which made him wonder about something else.

"Why three detectives?"

"They said they came to take another statement from you, but it's more likely that they came to arrest you no matter what was said."

Shawn looked up, startled. He'd forgotten Harris was still in the room, and he hadn't even realized that he'd asked the question aloud.

"From what I've heard, the reason there are three of them is because of the injuries your fiancée received. They were told you were a big man and would probably resist. To be honest, looking at Mr. Canker, I think he was hoping you would."

"They really do believe it was me who hurt Rosie?" he asked in a quiet voice, almost to himself rather than to Harris. The more he thought it, the more he believed it.

A firm hand pressed down on Shawn's shoulder. "We will sort this out, mate."

Chapter 9

A few hours later Belle was going out of her mind. She had paced around the Alpha's house continuously. Eventually, not being able to take it anymore, she called one of the other enforcers to take her place. Screw it. If Harris wanted to demote her or punish her, she would take it.

Making sure Larry was in place and happy, she marched toward the village police station. Felix was lounging outside, leaning against the wall with his arms crossed over his chest. He saw her coming and moved to stand in front of the door.

She held up her hand toward him when he opened his mouth "Don't even fucking start."

"He isn't going to be happy, Belle." She knew he meant Harris.

"What does he expect? That's my mate in there." She pointed behind him. "If that was your mate in there, would you stay away? Would you let her be questioned for hours for something she didn't do?"

Felix's stance relaxed a little as the question began to penetrate his brain. A few seconds later he moved aside, but placed a hand on her shoulder before she fully passed him. "Go careful, okay?"

With a nod, she pushed the door open and walked into the building. She heard the voices coming from Garrett's office.

"I didn't hit her. No matter how many times you ask the

answer won't change." Shawn's desperate voice, which was tinged with anger, hit her first.

How far had he been pushed in those few hours in that small room? She stormed toward the room, but before she reached the door it flew open and Harris was standing there. She stopped when he stepped forward and closed it behind him.

"Belle," he growled.

"Alpha." She lowered her head a notch. "He's my mate. Please."

"There's nothing you can do right now."

"I can be here as some kind of support. How long are you going to let them question him for something he hasn't done?"

Harris stepped toward Belle and placed a hand on each of her shoulders. "It's nearly over. Shawn has actually done well, although he grew upset. I can honestly say he has a couple of champions in that room. Out of the three that came, only one is stubborn enough to not yet accept that he's innocent. But the other two are growing tired with the lead detective."

"Harris, please let me in there." Belle knew the answer was going to be no, but she had to try.

Her Alpha sighed deeply and shook his head. "Sit there." He pointed to a chair just outside the room. "And don't move 'til it's over."

His voice left no room for argument, his face stern, but still she offered a little resistance. She just couldn't help herself.

"I'm not a child." She really wanted to stomp her foot like

the petulant child she felt like, but his response was a low, deep growl that lifted the tiny hairs on her arms and the back of her neck. She sat in the chair without another peep.

Harris turned his huge body and walked back into the room. The voices inside went quiet for a few minutes before starting up again.

"Mr. Burr, I'm going to ask for the last time—do you still deny causing the injuries to your fiancée?"

"Yes. I did not lay a finger on Rosie. When Rosie left the house that night I was lying on the floor bleeding, unable to do anything. And no, I didn't beat her up before she stabbed me in defense. She stabbed me in anger because someone at her work pissed her off," Shawn's tired voice replied.

"I think we should end this today, gentlemen." Harris spoke up. "Mr. Burr has answered all of your questions…repeatedly."

"You have no jurisdiction here, Mr. Rockwell. The only reason you are here is because I allowed it."

Belle inwardly snorted. Harris was not going to like that. This was his village, and these were his people.

"*Mr. Canker.*" Harris's voice was soft but deadly, even Belle would have cowered if she'd been in the room. At that particular moment she wished she was a fly on the wall to see what Mr. Canker's face looked like. "I will say this again—this is my village. If you wish to question Mr. Burr any more, not only will we do this officially, a lawyer will be called to his side. You have had him in here for hours without arresting him, which means he is able to walk out of this room. You have also asked the same questions over and over and received the same answers. Even before reading any witness statements and medical info you have in your files, I can tell you he is innocent."

"It doesn't matter what you think, *Mr. Rockwell*. We need to get to the bottom of what happened to both parties."

"Detective Canker, are you going to be arresting Mr. Burr today?" Garrett asked formally.

After a moment's silence the voice that Belle assumed to be this Canker person spoke up again. "Can we have a few minutes together, please?" he asked.

Belle heard the shuffling of feet and movement of chairs before Garrett's office door opened and three suited men left the room. Belle stood and immediately sought out her mate. She rushed into the room, past both her Alpha and Garrett, and threw herself into Shawn's arms, wrapping around him in a tight hug.

"Belle?" he said, his voice sliding over her like a silk glove. "You shouldn't be here."

A grumbled agreement came from Harris as he and Garrett left the room and walked down the hallway. Belle shrugged her shoulders. Nothing was keeping her from her male at this precise moment. She shut the door, leaving her and her mate inside the office alone.

"I needed to be close to you. It's been hours. I hate the fact that they have treated you like a criminal."

"They have to get the facts straight. Rosie walked into an

accident-and-emergency with broken bones and bruises and told them I had done it."

A low growl started in her throat and slipped from between her lips. Anger boiled deep in her veins.

"Hey." Shawn pulled her back from his chest and looked down at her, his hands still resting on her hips. "I'm still here. Although at first the world dropped from under my feet, I did nothing but tell the truth." He lowered his voice so only she could hear. "As shifters we live by fate—our mates, our lives, it's all planned out before us and we live it. If this was meant to be… I met you, didn't I?"

The smile that lifted his lips lifted his eyes too. Her heart danced. Was he finally accepting her?

"I'm still alive and here with you now." He whispered the words and lowered his head to plant a kiss on her lips. She licked them afterward, hoping to taste his flavor.

"But what if they take you away?" she asked, fear lacing her voice.

"Then I'm sure you won't be far behind." He lowered his head and his lips touched hers briefly. When he pulled back, she could see the sincerity of his words.

That brief, touching moment was broken when the office door swung open. One of the men who'd left earlier stood looking at them with a frown.

"Something going on between you two?" he asked.

"She's here supporting me as a friend," Shawn said, leaping

to their defense.

He wasn't lying as such, just leaving the *mate* details out. The copper wouldn't understand anyway. Belle was glad the man hadn't seen the sweet kiss Shawn had given her. That could have created another whole load of problems for her mate.

"Grown close, have we, Mr. Burr?" he asked, looking down at the hand Shawn still had on one of her hips. Shawn's hand dropped from her body to his side.

"Does asking snide questions come with the job?" Belle asked, turning and standing in front of Shawn protectively.

"Back down, Belle. Don't go screwing things up." Her Alpha's voice slid into her mind.

Looking over the detective's shoulder, Belle saw Harris step into view, his gaze firmly fixed on her. She wanted to hiss and growl at the offensive copper, but chose to honor her Alpha.

"Can he leave?" she asked, trying hard to keep the displeasure out of her voice.

Looking at Shawn, the man said, "We have decided to suspend the questioning for now. However, I'm sure we'll be back at some point. Don't leave the village, and make sure you're available for more questioning." With that the man turned on his heel and joined the other men in the reception area, then they left the building together.

Shawn's hand touched her shoulder, gripping it lightly. It was then Belle realized she'd taken a step after the detective, wanting to knock his block off.

"Belle…"

She swiveled around at the sound of her mate's voice. Before she managed to open her mouth to ask what he wanted his lips covered hers.

Chapter 10

Shawn watched the obnoxious copper walk out of the building. When Johnathon had come back into the room and Belle had stood in front of Shawn, a whole array of thoughts and feelings had gone through his mind. At first he'd questioned if she'd done it because of her job or because she was his mate. Annoyance took over for a few seconds; shouldn't he be the one protecting her? Then worry had crossed his mind when Belle had taken a step to go after the detective. He'd quickly, but lightly, touched her shoulder and curled his fingers softly around it, stopping her from going after the man. All at once he accepted fate and his mate, where he was and the position he was in.

"Belle…" He left the rest of his sentence unsaid, because when she turned he did what he wanted to do; fuck whatever came after. Seeing her rosy lips, he lowered his head and kissed her.

Her flavor fueled his fever for her. Tongues explored, tastes swapped, and Shawn's cock enlarged to a painful point. He wanted inside of his mate, he wanted to stroke his fingers along her skin, to suck her pert breasts into his mouth. His hands reached behind Belle's head, pulling her closer as their lust drove higher. Pheromones filled the small room, pushing their passion.

His hands lowered down her body until they were just underneath her butt. He lifted her, and she wrapped her legs tightly around his waist. The world ebbed away until it was just the two of them. Her sounds, her scent, filled him.

She began grinding her pussy against his stiff shaft, sending small shocks down his dick and to his balls. He needed to get inside of his mate. His tiger roared in agreement. He needed some kind of surface to lean against. He had to remember the layout of the room they were in, but her hands began roaming underneath his shirt. Soft, silky hands combined with long, raking nails. Could he get any harder?

Belle pulled away, leaving them both breathless. "Are you going to fuck me or just stand there?" she asked with a gleaming twinkle in her eyes.

"I'm going to be so far inside you—"

"Not in my bloody office you aren't!" Garrett stood red-faced in the open doorway.

Shock rippled through Shawn as everything came back to him. For a few precious seconds while he'd had his hands on Belle he'd forgotten where they were and why. He lowered Belle to the floor, depression hitting him like a ton of bricks, and he wished that he could get that peaceful existence back. He'd never lost control with Rosie like he had done just now. He would have fucked Belle against the wall and not given a shit if Garrett had walked in on them or not.

"Oh God, Garrett, I'm so sorry," he whispered, looking down at the floor, unable to meet the man's eyes. Embarrassment overtook any other emotion he had at that point.

"Don't you dare reprimand him, Garrett." Belle's fierce voice filled the air. "He isn't a kid, and you have no idea what it is like to be with a true mate."

Shawn winced at her harsh words. He had never known what it was like to be with one until he'd seen Belle.

Garrett paled, taking a step back as if he'd been struck.

"Low blow, Belle," Harris growled, stepping up behind the portly village copper.

Although Belle immediately bowed her head to their Alpha she mumbled in defiance, "Well, he doesn't."

"Shawn, I'd advise you to take your mate home before she places more of her foot in her mouth."

Nodding, Shawn tugged his mate with him as quickly as he could and left Garrett's office.

As they hit the fresh night air Belle pulled out of Shawn's hold. "Do I embarrass you?" she asked. Her cheeks were tinged with a red blush, anger written all over her face. Shawn also scented pain coming from her.

He noticed the detectives' black SUV was still parked outside with the men sitting in it. "Can we not do this here?" He whispered low enough for Belle to hear while motioning to the car with his eyes.

"Crap," she cursed and began walking down the street. When she realized he wasn't following she turned and lifted her eyebrows in a questioning manner. "Are you coming, Burr?"

Shawn followed her through the village until they reached his place.

Standing outside his door, Belle asked him again, "Do I

embarrass you?"

He frowned, shaking his head. "Why would you think that?"

"You dropped me faster than a bad habit in Garrett's office, and then you couldn't drag me out of the building fast enough when Harris told you to take me home."

Shawn nearly laughed. Was this woman serious? Although he felt a little annoyed at being asked such a stupid question he pulled the emotion close inside him. Closing his eyes, he took a deep breath, then opened his eyes again.

"Garrett nearly walked in on us having sex in his office. Don't you think he has the right to be annoyed?" he asked. "And as for our Alpha asking me to take you home… Yes, I pulled you out of there pretty fast because, if you are honest, you'd admit that you do have a tendency to open your mouth and put your foot in it."

As he waited for her reply he walked into his home, all the time praying she wouldn't bite his head off. He was just being truthful. *She isn't Rosie,* he repeated to himself over and over again. He was pleased when she followed him inside, a thoughtful look on her face. He watched the cogs spinning around in her head before a huge smile broke out across her beautiful face.

"I do, right? Felix is always telling me to bite my tongue, and as for sex in Garrett's office… Ewww… That man needs better hygiene, we could have caught something in there."

Shawn stood there in shocked silence while Belle went to the fridge and opened the door to look inside.

"What are we going to make for tea? I'm starving."

That was her answer? After he'd told her she had a big mouth, or at least one that got her into trouble, she wasn't going to shout at him? If he had uttered anything like that to Rosie, he would have been in for a night of pain. Again he had to remind himself that Belle wasn't Rosie.

"Whatcha standing there with your mouth open for? Looks like you're catching flies."

Shutting his mouth with a snap, Shawn walked toward her and wrapped an arm around her waist. "Thank you," he said, kissing her cheek.

"For what?" she asked, turning in his arms.

"For being you," he replied before kissing her mouth.

He drove his tongue between her lips and stroked it along hers. She tasted divine. The arousal he'd felt in Garrett's office returned tenfold. Picking her back up under her butt, he pushed the refrigerator door shut with her body and leaned them both against it, his mouth never leaving hers.

Fire boiled in his veins; it was as if every single emotion bubbled as one and turned into passion. His cock was rigid and now pressed against her heated core. He wanted to pound into Belle, to fuck her senseless. A soft moan from Belle vibrated along his tongue.

"Oh God, you're driving me nuts," he said, pulling away from her lips to speak.

"Then fuck me. Take your passion and show me what you got."

If he could make their clothes disappear with a thought, they would both be stark naked right now. Slowly, he lowered his mate to the floor with a grin on his face. "How about we make this fun?"

He took a step back from Belle and began ripping at his clothes. Buttons dinged as they hit glass, wood, and whatever else. Following suit, Belle did the same, revealing her gorgeous body. Moving around her while trying to struggle out of his jeans, Shawn opened the front door and watched Belle's face fill with confusion. But when he shifted his tiger stood still and saw understanding drift through his mate's eyes. Taking off toward the moors, Shawn's tiger ran.

* * * *

Oh, her mate was crafty. Belle watched his orange and black stripes disappear through the front door before she even started her shift.

In her haste, her jeans wrapped around her ankles, making her topple over. "Fuck this," Belle mumbled after falling to her hands and knees, annoyed she'd been caught off-balance.

Quickly, she shifted, feeling the muscles alter and bones crack. The jeans once caught around her ankles fell off her now palm-sized paws.

Her hearing, eyesight, and sense of smell increased. The sweet aroma of her mate filled her nostrils, and her cat's womb fluttered with excitement. It was dark outside now, but with her feline eyesight she could just make out the rear end of Shawn's tiger in the distance. Her tiger lifted her head and roared into the night, then took off, following her mate.

Belle's tiger moved slowly between the trees just on the outskirts of the village. The woods weren't very big, but sizable enough for two huge tigers to play amongst. Belle sat back in her tiger's mind, watching the scene play out.

The scent of their mate wound around the large, several-hundred-years-old trees; he'd run around a few of them, rubbing his scent over the bark. She crouched low as his unique bouquet became stronger. He was close. Her ears twitched, listening for any kind of sound, but all she could hear were the crickets, a mouse not far in the distance, and several birds in the trees.

At the sound of a twig snapping she jerked her head to the right, looking behind a fallen tree. Crouching even further, she stilled, waiting... Nothing. Was he behind the tree? Was he lying close to the ground, waiting for her to make a move?

Taking a chance, she drew her leg muscles tighter, ready to pounce, when pain—not enough pain to cause her anger, but enough to know her mate had found her—from the male tiger pouncing on her had her rolling onto her back and striking out with her paws. She heard the sound of a deep, rumbling growl from above. All she could see were the back and orange stripes of her mate standing astride her, then his tongue swept over her jawline and his purr filled the air.

She flipped her large, muscled body over and swept her tail to the side of her torso, offering herself, and within seconds she was impaled on his cock.

Chapter 11

After their fun, both tigers curled up with each other and slept. Belle felt, then heard Shawn shifting into his human form. Following suit, Belle pushed through her shift, and just as she finished, she was met with the most gorgeous pair of crystal light blue eyes looking down at her. Shawn straddled her body so close his chest pushed against her breasts.

"Now that's a sight for sore eyes," he murmured, looking down between their bodies. He nuzzled her neck and inhaled deeply. "Mmm, you smell like nature wrapped up in a bundle of wild daisies and honey."

His words rippled through Belle like a silk glove. She closed her eyes, relishing the feel of his skin and the sound of his voice. She lifted her hands and wrapped them around his neck, her fingers caressing his warm skin. "No, *you're* a sight for sore eyes."

Pulling his head down, she kissed his lips. She gained entrance to his mouth, slipping her tongue inside. A duet of moans came from both of them. Belle could feel Shawn's thick, hard erection press against her lower stomach. Her hips jutted up as if they had a mind of their own, seeking pleasure against her clit. Shawn moved and Belle whimpered when she received what she sought.

She lifted her legs and wound them tightly around his waist. When his cock slid over her engorged nub she groaned. She could feel the thick vein, and each of the small ripples as she glided along his shaft, leaving his shaft damp with her dew. She could feel the velvet contrast against his iron rod.

She was finally going to lose her virginity to the man who it was meant for. She'd played with vibrators and such, so she didn't have a hymen, but not one man had ever placed anything inside her, that she'd saved for her mate.

Shawn's mood quickly changed, and he moved faster, almost as if he was frenzied. His hands roamed over her breasts, squeezing and caressing them to a point where she felt nips of pain, which added to her excitement. Her honey seeped from her pussy more, and it ran down the crack of her arse cheeks. She was so close and they were merely dry humping.

Belle moved her hands down, raking her fingers along Shawn's back, knowing that they were leaving red welts behind. He groaned loudly and pressed his hips against hers. The vibration of his rumbled groan surged through his tongue and rippled along hers.

Belle pulled her face away from his and looked into his blue eyes, panting for breath. She felt a tinge of guilt, because she knew he was still getting over his past; were they moving too fast? Was he going to mate her then spent an eternity feeling he had portrayed that fucking ex of his?

"Wait a sec." She moved her hands up to his chest and placed them, fingers splayed, on his very fine pecs. "You've been through a lot in the past week or so, and this…" She motioned between them. "…is going to happen at some point, but I don't want to have you rush in and then feel guilty about it."

Shawn frowned, a perfect crease dipping in between his eyebrows. "Shouldn't I be asking you that?"

"Huh?" Why would he be asking if she would feel guilty if they mated?

"Well… You know the police don't like me. They want to throw me into a deep, dark, dank cell for beating on a woman—"

Belle couldn't let him finish. It broke her heart thinking of him being put away for something he was innocent of. She lifted her head and entwined her hand behind his neck and pulled him down. Their lips met in the middle and began another damp but hot dance.

"I won't let them take you away. Mate me. Make me forever yours no matter what happens," she pleaded with him mentally.

Shawn halted their heated kiss and pulled back to look into her eyes. His head lowered until his forehead was touching just underneath her chin. What was going through her mate's mind? He pulled even further away from her to turn over and rest on his back, an arm thrown over his eyes.

"Oh God, what if they do arrest me? Rosie has already proved she can be manipulative enough to get herself beaten up to blame me."

Belle could hear the pain and the scent of the emotion surrounded her mate. She knew he was innocent. She wished humans had the ability to scent emotion. It would make things so much easier. She couldn't imagine Shawn being placed in a cell for something he didn't do. In her wildest dreams it couldn't happen…could it?

"We won't let that happen. You aren't going anywhere. This is home now, and one way or another, we will make this work. You have to believe. We have to…"

Her gaze roamed up and over his handsome body. His long, lean but muscled legs. His hard, thick shaft that rested on his lower stomach. She wanted to grasp it and feel him writhe as she pumped it, to watch the look on his face when he came. His well-defined six-pack. His chest that had a fine dusting of black hair. Her mate moved his arm and looked up at her, his clear crystal blue eyes shimmering under a film of tears.

She placed an open palm on his cheek and caressed it. "I'm with you all the way, no matter where it takes us."

"It will just cause you pain if we mate and I'm taken away." His hand rested over the top of hers on his cheek. "To go years witho—"

"No!" she interrupted. She'd had enough of the negative thoughts. She straddled his hips, grinding her damp pussy over his cock, and lowered her head to place nibbling kisses on his lips. "You have to have faith. You didn't do anything." She stroked her hands over his pecs, loving the feel of them under her palms. "Innocent…" she said, laying a kiss on his lips again.

"You know that, but they don't."

"They will," she insisted.

"But what if—"

"No, no, no. For God's sake, man…We can't think like that. Inn-o-cent," she ground out again. "Believe."

Shawn closed his eyes and sighed. Belle waited with bated breath and hoped that when he opened his eyes again, she would see belief in them. She wanted to growl, to howl at the whole situation.

Not wanting to wait any longer, she slammed her lips down on his and ground her pussy against his still rock hard shaft. Lifting up a little, she grabbed hold of his cock and began pumping, feeling the difference between the soft and hard—the velvet skin moving against the hard muscle underneath. With his groan and the bucking of his hips Belle knew she had his undivided attention now. No more stalling. No more *ifs* and *buts*. This time she was going all out to get what she wanted, and even with his reservations, she knew he wanted it too.

Shawn hissed through his teeth when she ran her thumb over the slit of his dick and lifted it to her mouth. She closed her eyes and groaned above him, tasting the musky, salty flavor of his pre-cum. With a buck of his hips and a roll Belle found herself underneath her mate, his blue eyes looking down at her filled with lust and…love?

* * * *

Belle's eyes shone back at him from below. She was beautiful. Shawn knew the time had come to make this woman his mate once and for all. Fuck Rosie and her family. Hadn't he put up with enough of their shit? Whatever was to come he would deal with it with Belle at his side.

Belle's hand was still grasped around his cock, and while he'd been looking down at her, she'd begun to pump it slowly up and down.

"Put it where it's supposed to be, but I can promise you this, the first time, will be fast, hard, and furious. I need inside you this very second." He jerked his hips, pushing his length inside her hand, and pulled it out, emphasizing his urgency.

He felt her warm, wet pussy at the tip of his cock where she positioned it, and he pushed slowly inside her. Belle arched her back, her legs wrapping around his waist. He groaned in unison with her as he embedded his shaft until his balls rested against her arse.

"No more procrastinating," he whispered into her ear and pulled out until the tip of his cock rested at her entrance. With a surge of his hips he was fully embedded once again.

A small, whimpered moan came from Belle's mouth. He began kissing and nibbling on her neck, working his way down to her breasts, all the time setting a frantic pace as old as time. His gums itched as his fangs withdrew, and he scraped them along the pulse in her neck, closing his eyes and breathing in her wonderful scent. Belle arched once again and moved her head to the side. She licked up the side of his pulse. He was really going to do this. He was really going to mate the woman meant for him. Not to just imprint, but to actually give a piece of his heart and soul to a woman who would love him just as much as he loved her.

"I promise to love you always, to never lay a hand on you in anger. You will be in my heart 'til the day I die. I have never felt this way before. It's you, Belle. My heart and soul have been waiting for you. Accept me and my flaws?"

"Always, my mate." Belle smiled, then licked up the side of

his neck.

An image of Rosie briefly flitted through his mind. He lifted his head enough to look down at Belle. Rosie disappeared—she didn't belong there any longer.

Unable to hold back, he thrust inside Belle deeply but slowly so he could feel every inch of his cock slipping inside her welcoming pussy. She was so tight. Picking up his momentum, he felt the coming orgasm pull his balls up close to his body, and he thrust hard and fast. Perspiration beaded his body. Licking up the pulse in Belle's neck, he again scraped his teeth along it.

"Come, my tigress." With a quick, hard jerk Shawn plunged one final time inside of Belle and bit down near her collarbone as she did the same to him.

He had never felt such an explosion of an orgasm as he did then. He felt the spurting of his life force pushing its way out the end of his shaft into Belle's waiting womb. Her blood coated his tongue. A feeling of being totally complete crossed his mind. It was as if he could feel both of their souls reaching out to entwine around each other.

Belle's teeth released his neck and she howled into the night as she reached her orgasm. Her pussy clenched around his shaft as if it trying to milk everything it could.

"I love you, my tiger. I knew you would find me," Belle panted into his ear.

Chapter 12

The night air was cool around them. At the moment, both tiger and man were content.

Belle had lowered the grip of her legs around his waist as she fell asleep, tucked up in his arms. Shawn brushed a curl off her forehead, looking over her angelic face as she napped. She had a fine coating of pale freckles on her nose. Her eyes flitted left and right under their lids. Her bow-shaped lips pursed every now and again as if something bothered her in her dreams. Her hair, although short and spiked, was currently giving her the just-fucked look.

She was so different from Rosie. She didn't give a shit if something was out of place in the house. One day before she visited he left dirty clothes laying around just to see what she'd do, and she hadn't even blinked.

His cock was again fully hard and ready to go. He run his fingers up and down her skin while she slept. He also nibbled on her breasts, making her stir. Then a thought came to him suddenly, stopping him from waking her up fully with his tongue wrapped around her clit. Her family. Crap, what would they think of him? He had no doubt they would believe him, because his scent would confirm his honesty. But what if they knew he could end up in prison, leaving her behind, mated and on her own?

He flinched when Belle's hand touched his face. He'd been so lost in the horrible thoughts of him incarcerated that he hadn't seen her move.

"What's put that terrible frown on your face, my tiger?"

He closed his eyes and leaned into her palm, seeking the heat and love it portrayed. "Your family…what will they think of me?" He couldn't add the thought about jail.

When he received no answer he opened his eyes to look at her. He saw the love she had for him glittering in her eyes.

"They will love you as I do. I have no doubt about that. I have a question though." A small frown appeared between her eyes. "Where are we going to live? My room at my parents is so small I can barely fit a double bed in there. It's a tight squeeze, but you would be more than welcome. Although…" She paused for a moment, seeming to contemplate something before continuing. "Sex would have to be a quiet affair. The walls are pretty thin, and of course, with our shifter hearing…" The words trailed off, but he could guess the rest of the sentence.

Shawn snorted, which led to a chuckle, then a full-blown belly laugh as his mate stared up at him with a what-the-fuck look.

"You…we…and… Oh my God." He couldn't talk. He was laughing so hard his stomach hurt. When he finally managed to calm down, he cleared his throat and started again. "Here I was wondering about your family and my situation. We have just mated, and I want my cock deep inside of you constantly, and you ask where we're going to live. I, umm, really do not want to be inside you when a bang from your parents comes through the walls… Oh God, can you imagine that?"

He cringed at the image of him being firmly embedded in his

mate, making her scream out, when her parents banged on the wall. Breakfast the next day would be an embarrassing affair for sure. He started laughing again, and this time Belle joined him.

"The flat Harris gave me is mine as long as I pay the rent, right?" he asked her.

"Yep."

"Then come live with me?" he asked. He'd lost everything he'd worked for, and now it seemed fate was handing it back to him with roses. Did he really deserve this?

"You deserve it and more," she said.

Did I say that out loud, he wondered, then he shook his head and pushed the thought away. "I'll race you home," he challenged.

Shawn stood up, and with a last look at his mate through his human eyes, he allowed his tiger to take the reins and shifted.

"Run, tiger, run." Belle smiled at him and began her shift.

Even though his tiger wished to see his mate in her form, he didn't. With a swish of his tail, he took off running.

* * * *

Belle watched the sunrise while she lay in her mate's arms in what was now their new home. She lay on her side with Shawn firmly curled up behind her, his arms wrapped around her like string on a parcel. They fit together like a jigsaw piece.

She'd contacted Harris and Felix, asking for a couple of days off, and also told them about her mating. After congratulating her, Harris gave her a week off for their honeymoon period, whereas Felix made her promise to see him at least an hour a day to go over beta shit—his words—being he didn't want to delay his trip for too long. She'd given him the option to give Chris the job instead of her, but he wouldn't have it. He said under no circumstances would he change his mind about offering her the post. She'd agreed to his terms.

She watched the sun hit their bed and begin its slide over her mate's skin. Since he'd shifted again, his bronzed skin showed no sign of any burns at all.

Her thoughts suddenly drifted to her mother. This wasn't the first time she'd not gone home for the night, but it was the first since her mother had become sick. Today she was taking Shawn to meet her family. She was excited, albeit a little worried too. Her mother had been struggling with her health recently. Shifters didn't often get sick, but for some reason her mother had started losing weight six months ago. First, she'd become house-bound, then bed-bound. Now her muscles had started to waste away.

Doc Ben had done numerous blood tests and examinations. He'd even sent her to the hospital in Yorkshire for scans. He'd come to the conclusion that it wasn't the human side of her mother that was ill. It was actually her tiger. He assumed it had a virus of some kind and he asked her mother to shift so he could get bloods done and sent them off to another shifter doctor in a big hospital in London. They were waiting for the results.

Guilt racked Belle. She suddenly wanted to be near her parents. Last night only the negative thoughts about living with her parents had come up. Yes, the walls were thin but...

"Shawn." Belle turned in her mate's arms to face him.

He looked so peaceful. His bruising was all gone, and his stomach wound had also healed. She ran her hand over his cheek, and as she rubbed it, his scent hit her nostrils. Along with his shaving cream and shower gel his aroma carried the scent of musky pine. Her nipples peaked and hardened, and her lady parts moistened in readiness for his cock to be inside her. This wasn't the time though.

"My tiger," she said loud enough for his sleepy eyes to open. His pupils dilated, and the smile on his face said it was the best morning wake-up he could have.

"Good morning, mate," he said and moved an arm from behind her so he could run a finger over her collarbone where his new mark was. Tilting her head toward his fingers, she relished the feeling of his skin on hers.

"I need to go home. I have an urge to be with my mother."

Shawn frowned with a silent question. She knew what he was wondering.

"No one has contacted me," she said. "It's just a feeling. My mother has been sick for a while. I also feel a little guilty that I didn't tell them I wasn't going home last night. I know I could phone them." She tapped her forehead. "But I want to see her."

"Shower first, and we can eat on the way," he suggested.

"That's it? You aren't going to ask why or what?"

"Why would I?" he asked, his voice full of wonder.

"Well, I thought you might want some of this," she teased,

getting up on her knees and skimming her hands down her naked body.

His jaw dropped open as he watched her hands travel over her body, and the sheet tented at his groin.

With a smirk on her face, she climbed from the bed and danced her way to the bathroom. "Shower?" she asked, laughing.

A low growl followed her. As she reached out to turn on the water, Shawn's hands grasped her waist.

"Tease." His voice rumbled against her neck, followed by a lick over her new mating mark. Tiny shocks crested over her nerve endings straight to her groin.

"Quick shower, remember?" she said, wishing she didn't feel an urgency to see her mother. She could contact her parents telepathically, but she knew they would just fob her off, saying everything was well even if it wasn't.

Shawn purred against her neck again, sending more delicious shots through her body. His hands gripped her waist, and he stepped forward, pushing her into the stream of water. "You have to be dirty before you can be clean."

Skimming his hands up her body, he molded his palms over her breasts and began rolling her hard, peaked nipples between his fingers. She squeezed her thighs tightly together. He licked and nibbled her neck, and her head dropped back onto his shoulder as she relished the delightful feelings he was sending through her body. *Quick shower*, she kept telling herself.

Turning around in her mate's arms, she began kissing him

furiously. He took over the kiss, and it became raw, primal, almost as if he was asking her to surrender to him. He plundered her mouth until they were both breathless. After pausing for a second she came out of the lust-filled haze and realized he was leaning her against the shower wall, his hands grasping her backside, and her legs were tightly wrapped around his waist.

"You make me forget myself," he said with a frown on his face.

"Huh?"

"When I was with Rosie I always had to be aware, always had to know what I was doing. With you I seem to lapse into moments of…just doing."

She didn't like being compared to his ex, and jealousy rose high. "I'm not her," she spat out, pushing against his chest.

"Wait." He gripped her tighter. His scent became pungent as fear blasted from every pore. "I didn't mean it like I was comparing. I'm sorry."

Belle stopped struggling to be free of his arms. Dammit, she had to give him a chance, he'd gone through enough shit. Pleading eyes looked straight into hers.

"What I meant was… When I kiss you or touch you I'm not watching myself, I can just do and not fear any consequence. Do you understand?"

She shook her head. "You just confused me more."

Shawn sighed deeply and lowered her legs. But his hands rose to touch the top of her shoulders, each of his thumbs caressing one side of her collarbone.

"When I first got together with Rosie I would lose myself in her, but as time progressed, I realized when I was with her I would be watching myself like in a third-party way. If I touched her, I was very aware. If I talked to her, I was careful. Everything was planned. Nothing was spontaneous like I am with you. This here…" He motioned around to the shower. "…would never have happened. When I touch you I don't have to plan, or watch what I do or say. I'm free."

Belle's heart thumped in her chest. To lose precious seconds when kissing someone so deeply was new to her. Shawn was the only one she let close enough to do so. She thought back before meeting Shawn, when she was at work, patrolling around the village. Her mind would sometimes drift off, thinking of her mate-to-be, or dreaming of a new flavored ice cream, only to find she'd strolled a few miles along her route automatically without thinking. For him to be constantly aware of what he did…wouldn't that be exhausting?

She noticed the tired wrinkles in the corners of his eyes. His lips that dipped lower at the edges as if in a state of constant unhappiness. She ran a finger over his face. Shawn purred and leaned his head into her hand.

"I'm not her, Shawn. You can be as free as you want with me." She smiled. "There is only one rule you need to remember."

He looked at her with questioning and worried eyes.

"Put the toilet lid down after you pee. Do you know what it's like to fall down the frigging toilet because someone left the lid up?

Arse down, legs up and flailing. Not fun." She giggled and was relieved when he joined her. "Now, my tiger, are you going to fuck me quick before we—" She moaned as Shawn's lips covered hers and his cock penetrated her.

Chapter 13

"Hey, Pop." Belle kissed her father's wrinkled cheek. He gave her a tight hug in return.

"Morning, sunshine. A bit of a late night?" he asked with a cheeky smile.

"Yeah, well…" She turned toward Shawn, who was nervously standing behind her. "This is the reason. Pop, meet Shawn Burr, my mate," she announced proudly.

Her father moved forward and greeted Shawn like he was family. Instead of taking the hand her mate held out, her father wrapped his arms around Shawn and hugged him like there was no tomorrow.

"Welcome to the family, son. If Belle hasn't already told you, I'm Barry. You treat her right, and we won't have any problems." Her father looked sternly at Shawn, his old, weathered face showing his age, but his body was still lean and muscled. He held his head high and stood up to the young man as if he were young himself.

"Sir, you'll have no problem. In just a short time she has become my world. I swear to you I would never lay a finger on her or treat her anything but right."

Her father nodded, then turned, walking into the kitchen.

"Pop, is Ma awake?"

"Aye, lass, go see her and take your young man with you."

Making sure Shawn followed her, Belle led the way through

the three-bedroom cottage. Since waking up this morning she wanted to ask Shawn if he wouldn't mind moving in there, and now that she was back in the house she was certain she couldn't move out.

Her parents had tried to have kits for many years. When they hit their forties Belle came along. Now in their seventies they were showing their ages, even for shifters. Shifters tended to keep their young looks, their bodies rippling with energy. Although when they hit their late nineties or early hundreds their bodies began to slow down a lot.

That reminded her of an elderly couple in the village who were jaguar shifters—May Turner was a hundred and fourteen and her mate Fred was a hundred and twenty. They were pretty much house-bound now. Not long ago they were being ill-treated by their landlord, a despicable cheetah shifter named Murphy Buzzell. The Alpha had taken him in hand, and now, with the help of the village, the couple were being well looked after in a house with free rent.

Reaching her parents' room, Belle gently knocked and walked inside. Seeing her mother propped up in bed and smiling made Belle's day. Rushing over to her, Belle placed a loving kiss on her cheek and hugged her gently.

"You look good today, Ma."

"It's a good day, dear." She tapped Belle's cheek then looked behind her. "Who's this then? The reason you stayed out?"

Heat rushed to Belle's cheeks. She felt like a kid being caught with her hand in the cookie jar. Standing, she pulled Shawn further into the room. Keeping hold of his hand, she introduced him.

"This is Shawn. My mate. Shawn, this is my ma, Constance Grant." Excitement filled her voice. She couldn't help it. Ever since fully mating him she felt waves of glee run through her. Just telling her mother made it happen all over again.

Shawn stepped forward and offered his hand, but her mother had other plans.

She tapped her cheek. "Plant one there, boy. It's been a while since a young man kissed me," she said, chuckling.

Shawn obliged with a smile on his face. It was so good to see her parents finally interact with her mate. It seemed like forever since she'd met Shawn.

"No other man will be kissing you while I'm around, except me," her father gruffly said, walking into the room. "Mine!" he growled possessively as he sat on the bed and kissed his mate's cheek.

Belle shook her head at her parents' antics. Her mother actually had a rosy tint to her pale cheeks and was smiling from ear to ear. It looked good on her. Belle sighed before asking the question she feared to. "Have you heard anything from Doc Ben?"

The smile that was on her father's face fell, and he looked down at the floor before lifting his gaze up to look at her. Tears welled in his eyes, making Belle draw a deep breath. Her heart seemed to die in her chest.

"Aye, lass, he came around briefly last night. Your mother's blood tests came back showing she was anemic, so he gave us a prescription for iron pills." He stopped as if that was the end and looked toward her mother. Belle knew her father; he was holding something back.

"What about her tiger's blood?" she asked.

And there it was…her father's face paled, and grief and pain could be clearly seen on his face. The scent of it began pouring from him as well as her mother.

When he didn't say anything, just looked over to his wife, Belle asked again. "Pop?"

It was her mother who answered. "He says my tiger has leukemia. It's very rare for a shifter animal to get sick. As you know, our combined lives results in us leading more energetic, healthy, and longer lives. But for some reason my tiger is pretty sick, and it's flowing through to me."

Belle's legs turned to jelly, and the world darkened at the edges of her eyesight. It suddenly seemed as if the room didn't have enough air in it. She felt Shawn's hands grip her waist, catching her as her legs buckled. It seemed as if every single cell in her body had stopped working except for the ones that created tears. Tears that pooled in her eyes and began falling down her face. She knew her mother had been sick for a while, but to think of her dying… Belle lived for her parents. What would she do without them?

"Tell me he can heal your tiger, Ma. Tell me everything will be okay." She moved out of Shawn's arms and knelt beside her mother's bed to grip her hands.

Her mother's voice dropped to a whisper. "I'm sorry, baby."

Belle couldn't breathe. She felt sick to her stomach. She

couldn't make sense of anything. Her brain felt like it was on fire, boiling with turmoil.

"No, no, no. Ma, no. I can't be without you. You are my world. What about Pop? He won't…can't… He will die along with you. Your souls belong to each other." Great big racking sobs began and grew in her chest. Tears poured down her cheeks. She gripped her mother's hands as if they were a lifeline and she could pull her away from the illness she had.

Belle closed her eyes, begging not to see her mother so sick. This wasn't happening. This couldn't be true. Behind her grief she felt the anger grow at such an injustice, and she wanted to blame someone for it.

* * * *

Shawn watched his mate fall to pieces at her mother's bedside. He'd been nervous about meeting Belle's parents, but after they had both greeted him like family he'd relaxed. However, now, after hearing their news and watching his strong woman fall apart, the world suddenly seemed like a darker place. All his problems drifted away; they were nothing compared to this.

He had felt the love in the room. The smiles on the family's faces, the subtle touches here and there. He'd caught the playfulness of Belle's mother. Although she was sick, she'd still asked him to kiss her cheek, knowing not only that her mate wasn't far from her but it would get a reaction from him too—even if Shawn was potentially family. That was before the grief had taken over. The scent of pain, loss, and even guilt overtook everything else. He wanted to go over to Belle, to scoop her up in his arms. He would plead, beg, or swap his life to any higher power, if there was one, to give this loving family more time together.

Belle's father lay a hand on his daughter's head while his females cried together. Shawn watched as a stray tear fell down the old man's face.

If Shawn's heart felt like it was gripped in a vise, what did Belle's feel like? His heart broke as he watched his mate sit by her sick mother's bed, clutching her hand and crying so hard her whole body was shaking.

He moved slowly forward to lift Belle into his arms, but she pushed him away, so he changed tactics and sat on the floor behind her. He tried to wrap his arms around her, hoping he could help comfort her in some way. Again she pushed him away. He began to worry. Why wouldn't she let him help her? Why did she keep pushing him away? He couldn't take her pain away, but he could offer some kind of comfort, but she wouldn't let him.

Taking a deep breath, he reminded himself that this wasn't Rosie, this was his mate. This was Belle, and she was hurting. She wasn't pushing him away destructively.

He thought back to when his parents had been killed. He'd wanted to scream and yell, he had wanted to punch, hit, or kick something. Most of all though, he had wanted someone to blame. Was that how Belle felt right now? Was she looking for someone to blame for her mother's impending death?

Shawn couldn't let his feelings of rejection rule him. If Belle needed someone to direct her grief onto, he would be there for her.

Mate hurting.

I know, my friend. Shawn sighed.

I help?

You know what, that actually might be a good idea.

Without another thought, Shawn began his shift, giving free rein to his other half. His eyesight became clearer. His hearing improved to the point he could hear the skittering of bugs around them. His clothes shredded, and fur threaded through every pore until finally Shawn's near seven-hundred-pound tiger stood in his place, shaking his fur out.

Without preamble, his tiger curled his huge body around his grieving mate's and tucked his head onto her lap. He purred lightly, letting her know he was with her in one form or another. He knew the vibration from his throat would echo along her skin even though it was covered in cloth. When one of Belle's hands lowered and gave a quick stroke behind his ear, he knew he'd done right in offering her comfort. Shawn's tiger purred a little louder in response.

* * * *

Almost two hours later the family—including Shawn—gathered in the kitchen. The air felt thick with grief.

"Why don't you youngsters go for a run?" Belle's father suggested. "Take your mind off things for a little while."

Shawn thought that was a good idea, but Belle shook her head.

"Your mother isn't dead yet, girl. Now go out there, take

your mate and run. Believe me, you will feel loads better."

Shawn saw the determination in her father's eyes, so when Belle looked at her father defiantly, he coaxed her himself.

"Come on, love, your dad is right." When she shook her head yet again, he tried to bait her. "My cat says you don't want to let his female out because he is faster anyway."

His beast was calling out to his female in Shawn's mind, as if she could hear him. He didn't like their mate feeling as bad as she did.

With a growl of annoyance, Belle rose from her seat and moved to the back of the house, where she undressed and shifted lightning fast. By the time Shawn was undressed, she had already disappeared into the trees.

Belle ran like there was a beast after her. She ran so fast and furiously that Shawn's tiger watched nothing but her cat's tail swish in aggravation while he ran behind her. Eventually he'd had enough of seeing her behind and decided it was time for his mate to let her anger loose another way. He gathered speed to catch up with her, and when he was within the space to pounce on her without injury, he did.

"What the fuck are you doing, or should I say what is your fucking beast doing?" Belle asked.

"My tiger has decided you and yours need to calm down, and instead of seeing your backside, he wishes you to lose your negative emotions another way. Blame him, not me," Shawn replied with a mental smirk.

He received a growl from both Belle and her cat. Within seconds Belle's cat flipped off Shawn's using the strength of her back legs and began circling her mate while showing her teeth and growling low.

"*Pissed much?*" Shawn taunted.

"*This is not the time to fucking piss me off…or my cat!*"

Although Shawn paused inside of his tiger's head at her answer, his cat continued to counter her cat's moves. Shawn, however, was suddenly thrown back into the past. Rosie shouting and screaming at him. Her hands slapping at his skin. Her feet and fists kicking and thumping. Her face red with anger. He couldn't do this again. Reaching out to his beast, he tried to rein it in.

We need to stop. We can't make her angry at us…at me. Please, Shawn begged.

This is our mate. It not the same as She Devil, his tiger argued. *Mate get bad news, she angry. She allowed.*

But… He knew his tiger was right, but what if it continued? What if this was the start to another abusive relationship?

Not happen! You believe mate will treat you bad?

Rosie didn't treat me bad at the beginning. Guilt swamped him when he'd realized he'd actually taunted Belle, his tiger had too. He'd never had the guts to do that before with Rosie. *We need to stop. This is all my fault.*

How your fault?

I started this… I let you start this… I added to it.

Let me take care of mate.

Shawn sighed and gave up trying to argue. Something inside of him knew that this wasn't the same thing. He was judging Belle on the grounds of a previous relationship. After spending time with her he knew deep down that she wasn't like Rosie.

Shawn's tiger struck, bringing Shawn out of his thoughts. He pounced on Belle's beast and dragged her to the ground. With flailing paws both tigers scrabbled together until the female was free and began circling him again. Shawn realized the female wasn't running.

She enjoying game. His tiger purred.

You no win, the female taunted.

Not answering her, Shawn's beast struck again. He bounded and landed on the back half of Belle's cat. Her legs failed and dropped to the floor, the weight of Shawn's cat keeping her down. The female feline bucked and rolled over, but Shawn's cat hung on for dear life. He was determined to win her submission.

For what seemed like forever the female fought, but gradually her muscles relaxed and a yowl ripped through the air. Immediately, Shawn's feline moved up and over the female, his teeth sinking into her neck. Shawn felt Belle's cat freeze, and victorious feelings flowed through his tiger.

I win. You mine. Shawn's tiger purred, sending vibrations through his mouth to the female below him. Her tail whipped to the side in the last act of defiance, then she relaxed totally underneath him.

Only because I let you.

Mine!

This time, the female replied before a purr ripped from her throat when her mate impaled her.

As the birds sang and the day continued, both tigers played, talked, and mated until finally a few hours later they walked home side by side in a relaxed manner. Both Shawn and his tiger could still scent the pain and grief rolling off their mate; it seemed to weigh down heavily on her. They didn't like it one bit, but there was only one cure for grief…time.

Chapter 14

The atmosphere was quiet and surly at Belle's parents' house as they all sat around the dinner table. Although her mother was ill, Belle's father had carried her to the table to join them in a meal. Even though her plate was barely touched she joined in the chatter and storytelling that her father started to break through the silence. It led to him telling Shawn a lot of the antics Belle had gotten into when she was younger. She knew her face was the color of a beetroot through some of the stories. As Shawn and her parents chuckled, Belle couldn't help but smile, and the atmosphere in the room warmed, becoming warm and toasty. This was what their normal mealtime had been like before her mother had gotten sick.

Belle watched her mother throughout the evening. She grew paler and paler until finally her father rose from the table and bid both her and Shawn goodnight. Picking his wife up in his arms, he walk toward their bedroom. Belle watched as they left the room. The love the pair still had for each other was in their eyes, the way her father carried his mate, his fingers caressing bare skin, and the occasional duck of his head when he kissed her.

"I want that," she said with awe, her heart fluttering.

She wanted to be loved as deeply as her father loved her mother. The love she had with Shawn was still so new. An image appeared in her mind of Shawn carrying her to their bed like that in fifty years' time. As her parents disappeared behind closed doors she looked toward her own mate.

"There's nothing stopping us from having that." Shawn, who'd been sitting beside her through their meal, moved closer and gathered her into his arms. She couldn't resist curling her body into his.

"You really think so?"

"Yep." He kissed the top of her head.

Looking up and into his eyes, she saw he wanted that too. She supposed coming out of a destructive relationship he would. "How can you want to be with me so quick after…you know, Rosie?" She watched sadness creep into his blue eyes, and they seemed to turn a shade darker.

He sighed, then said, "First off, I think being you are my fated mate, it was hard to resist. When I first spotted you it was love at first sight. Your body, your eyes, your tiger. Everything called out to me, but with Rosie so fresh in my mind, I tried to push you away. You, however, are quite persistent and wouldn't stay away." He chuckled, his eyes sparkling. "I'm glad you didn't," he said and gently laid a whisper of a kiss to her lips. "As shifters we know who our other half is. With Rosie it was different. It was lust at first sight. But even though I grew to love her, my tiger didn't. It was hard work. I did love her at first, but then I suppose fear of being alone and never meeting 'the one' kept me with her. I know if I had left her, her brothers would have handed me my arse. But it was a beating I would…could have taken. I might even have laid them out. But the fear of actually taking a beating…well, it's massive." Shawn sighed deeply. "I never even introduced my tiger to her, and I couldn't even if I had wanted to, because he slept, hiding away, because he strongly disagreed with who I had chosen. I think the reason I stayed with Rosie was for company. I hated being on my own. I know now if I had left her, my beast would have spoken more to me, but at that time I didn't know that."

"That's what I don't understand." Belle twisted in his arms to look at him properly. "You had a choice, you could have left her at any time. Why put yourself through so much?"

Belle wanted to understand, she needed to know. It was something that had niggled at her ever since she'd met him. He was a shifter, so he had more strength than an average human. He could have walked away from that relationship if he'd wanted to before it ended as it did.

"It had been so long since my beast had spoken to me I felt incredibly lost. I had nothing really. She took care of the money, the bills. Even the car I drove was in her name. By the time I realized she had control over everything that happened in my life, it was too late to stop it. It got so bad that I thought I'd done something so wrong that fate was telling me I wasn't entitled to a happily ever after."

"But you could have left, just taken a few clothes maybe. You could have fought her for your money." Feelings of frustration grew inside her. Why hadn't he left her? Why hadn't he fought for himself?

She could feel Shawn begin to withdraw, the metaphorical space between them growing. She could feel the waves of frustration grow from him as well as the scent of pain.

"If I could explain it, I would," he replied, his voice upping a notch in volume. "I loved her in the beginning. But over time I felt worthless, like I deserved it. When you're in the situation you can justify everything that happens. Now? I don't know, I feel stupid explaining why I stayed so long. I feel like an idiot for letting her hit me and abuse me. A couple of times I held her wrists to stop her from hitting me, but she always accused me of wanting to hit her. She would say I was the one abusing her. 'What do you want to do, hit me?' She'd repeat it over and over until I felt guilty for trying to stop her." Shawn growled low, running his hands through his hair. "Sometimes I did want to hit her back, or just slap her to make her stop. But I knew that would make things a whole lot worse."

Belle could see, let alone scent and feel, the boiling anger inside him. He wanted to lash out. For some reason she wanted him to; she wanted him to get angry, to allow his pain out. It was like watching a ticking bomb.

Shawn's hands paused on top of his head, his fingers tangled in his hair. It was like whiplash to watch so many emotions flicker through him. One moment she felt the boiling lava of anger inside him, then he raised his walls and…nothing. It was like he'd shut down.

"Defeated. That's how I felt." He slumped in his seat, his hands wringing together in front of him. "In the end, it was as if I wanted her to take my pain away…to kill me."

A lone tear dripped over his eyelid to fall down his face.

Belle raised a hand and covered his cheek with her palm, the tear stopped by her thumb.

"I couldn't even do it myself. Every time I picked up a blade or I even thought about suicide... I just couldn't do it." His whole body shook with emotion. He looked crushed. It was as if his admittance for wanting to die had killed part of his soul. Belle couldn't stand watching her mate in so much pain.

They ours, her tiger reminded her. *My mate hurt too for leaving him on his own for so long.*

We will help them mend, Belle vowed to her cat.

With a mental firm nod from her beast, Belle wrapped her hands around Shawn's biceps and tugged him toward her. At first he resisted, but with determination to help her mate, she persevered until she won out and he rested his head on her chest. Once he settled, she hugged him around his shoulders, holding him as tightly as she could.

"No more wanting to die, right?" She could feel her own tears sliding down her cheeks. To think of her mate in so much pain then and now hurt her too. She wanted him to live, not just for her, mainly for himself.

Shawn didn't answer or move.

"Right?" she asked more firmly. She felt him nod. Tucking her face into his neck, she pulled his spicy scent deep into her lungs. "It's okay. I have you now," she whispered in his ear.

Belle had no idea how long they sat together at her parents' table, holding each other. Gradually the room became darker. She knew she still had a question to ask Shawn. Sitting up straight, she pushed Shawn away slightly to look at his face.

She grimaced a little, wondering what his answer would be. "Um, would you mind staying here… I mean as in…living here?" She looked down toward her lap. "I don't want to leave my mum, with her being so sick."

"Hey." Shawn's slid a finger under her chin, lifting it up. Sorrow still filled his eyes, but so did compassion. "We are in this together, right?" He smiled. "If we were homeless and had to live in a box, I would do it. Sweetheart, I would follow you to the moon and back."

Wrapping her arms around his neck, she hugged him. "This place has thin enough walls for cardboard city." She giggled.

"Come on," Shawn said, urging her to stand up. "Let's get cleaned up and head to bed. Then perhaps I'll fuck you…albeit very quietly. We can get my stuff tomorrow. There isn't much, so it won't take a lot of time."

"It's a good plan." With one last hug and a quick kiss, she released her man and started collecting the dinner dishes from the table.

* * * *

The next morning Belle and Shawn were sitting at the table eating breakfast when her father walked in. Belle felt the wariness slip into Shawn, and his muscles stiffened, waiting for some kind of response from her father. Her father smiled at the pair of them, and Shawn promptly relaxed.

"Morning, Pop," Belle said, rising and kissing her father on the cheek.

"Just getting some coffee for your ma and me. How'd you both sleep?" he asked.

"We slept good," Belle replied. "How did Mum sleep?"

"Up and down, babe. The weather looks good this morning, and she wants to sit in the garden for a bit today, so I'm gonna take her outside later."

"We're going to take a walk back to Shawn's to pick his stuff up. We won't be long. Then, with it being Sunday, I'll cook us a roast." Sundays were important to her family, it was a day they spent together. No work, no patrols, nothing. After sleeping late, Belle and her mother would cook a large Sunday roast together. Afterward, when they were all stuffed and happy, they'd watch a movie or go for a stroll.

"You're picking Shawn's stuff up why?" her father asked, pausing from spooning coffee into two cups.

"We're going to stay here, Pop, with you and Mum. I can—"

"Hey now, love," Belle's father interrupted her. "You don't have to stay here. You are newly mated, and Shawn has his own place, right?" Her father sat down beside her, taking her hand in his.

"Pop, I want to stay here. Shawn says he's okay with it. Please." The word *please* came out as a small whine.

Her father's weathered, tanned hand squeezed hers. "Sweetheart, you are newly mated. Your mum is going to be sick no matter where you are. I'm still sturdy enough to take care of her. Do you think your mother would want you here when you should be with your mate?" He winked at both of them. "Get your bag packed and go stay with your mate, dear girl. We are okay. You will come by every day anyway, I know you. Your mother will want this. Believe me."

Belle shook her head in defiance. "No, I can't. I don't—"

"Belle Rosemary Grant, you listen to me."

Belle felt Shawn stiffened beside her. Her father noticed and sent a stern look his way too.

"Not now, boy, this is between my daughter and me. If you have something to say, I'll hear you out afterward." Turning back to Belle, her father continued. "Your mother and I wanted a big family, but when we reached our forties and hadn't gotten pregnant, we didn't think we could have any kits. Then out of nowhere you came along." Her father's voice began to get softer as he became lost in his memories. "You were our blessing, sweetie. But we also knew we had more years on us than the average parent. We made sure we brought you up well enough to withstand what life could throw at you. That's including if anything ever happened to one of us." He motioned to himself then jerked his thumb toward the hallway, indicating her mother. "Now, as I said, I'm still able to take care of your mother. But we want you to live your life. Go be with your mate where you can..." Her father cleared his throat and a tinge of red appeared on his cheeks. "...do what you do without having to worry about your parents' ears, if you get what I mean."

It was Belle's turn to blush. Had her father heard them last night? Bloody shifter hearing. How embarrassing.

She'd tried to be quiet. Shawn had taken her from behind, and it felt like his dick slid even deeper into her than before. He'd placed a palm on the small of her back, pushing her down and then lifting her hips. He'd moved in long, slow strokes until both of their orgasms built to the point she'd slammed her face into the pillow and screamed into it as her orgasm rushed through her.

Her father cleared his throat again, bringing her out of those delicious thoughts. Oh shit, now her father could smell something else.

Chapter 15

Embarrassment wasn't a strong enough word for what Belle felt right then, standing in her parents' kitchen thinking about sex. She was turned on, and her father was right there! He cleared his throat and averted his gaze away from her.

"Sorry, Pop," she whispered.

With a 'I've been there but don't want to know my daughter is' smile, he patted her hand and went back to making the two cups of coffee. After a quick stir, he dropped the spoon on the counter and picked up the mugs. He sent her another smile and nodded.

"It's time, sweetie. Every parent brings their child up to leave the nest one day. You, my dear, need a bit of a push. Your mum and I will be okay, and if not, we will shout. And as I said, I'm sure not one day will go by that you won't walk through that door while we are here."

Tears welled up in Belle's eyes, making everything look blurry. She knew her father was right, but the thought of not being there hurt like hell. "I love you, Pop," she said, her voice breaking.

"I love you more, my girl. That will never change." And with that her father walked down the hallway to his bedroom.

Belle stood and started to step forward after her father, but warm arms enclosed around her waist. She wondered how her father could just walk away after saying it was time for her to leave home. Wasn't he hurting? Did he really want her to go or was he just saying that? She growled in frustration. She wanted to go after him and argue.

"I wish I could climb in his head and know what he's thinking. He's telling me it's time to move out, and yet he knows my mother doesn't have long to live. How can he tell me to walk away?"

Shawn squeezed her a little tighter. "He isn't telling you to walk away, sweetheart. He's trying to make sure you have a life besides them."

Belle pushed his arms away from her waist and spun to face him, her anger rising like lava out of an exploding volcano. "What if I want to be here? What if I want to be around in case they need something? What if I don't want to move out?" Her voice rose the more she continued.

She wanted to rant. It was as if everything since learning her mother was dying wanted to break out from her. She paced, turning back and forth, her mind going over everything. She couldn't seem to stop.

"Belle!" Her father's shout brought her back to her senses.

She turned to see her father looking at her, his whole posture showing he was pissed. She hadn't even heard or seen him approach. Shit, had she been ranting away that badly? Oh God, he would have heard everything too.

Without a word he pointed toward Shawn. She turned, and a gasp left her when she saw her mate standing stiff as a board in fear. His hands were fisted at his side, his face as white as a sheet. His eyes clouded over with pain, he looked lost in the memories of his past. Immediately, she looked around to see what the fuck had scared him; she was ready to beat the shit out of them. A moment passed before she realized it had been her. Her ranting had sent Shawn into the turmoil he was in now. Her anger suddenly abated.

"I… Oh my God, I'm sorry. I…I didn't…" All she had wanted to do was vent her own anger. It had just happened, she hadn't planned it, she had just wanted to scream.

Looking at her mate now, her heart filled with sorrow and regret. Was Shawn always going to be like this? Was he always going to be scared when her voice rose?

Mate needs us.

But I caused this, what if he pushes me away?

Just go hug, kiss, or mate him. We will help him get past the bad. Make new and happy memories. Her tiger made it sound so simple.

Belle stepped toward him and gently laid a hand on a tightly coiled arm muscle. He flinched enough that she pulled her hand back, only to replace it again. This time he didn't recoil.

"Shawn," she said quietly. "Shawn, I'm sorry."

He didn't move, he didn't even blink. What was she to do? She looked toward her father, seeking his advice.

"Just keep talking to him. Skin-on-skin contact will help."

She turned back to Shawn, looking up at him. Her mouth felt like it was full of fur. Licking her dry lips, she tried to reach her mate mentally. "*Shawn, I'm so sorry. I didn't think. Fuck, I'm such a screw up.*"

He didn't move.

Belle sighed, but kept contact with him. She couldn't give up. No, she wouldn't give up on him. He was her mate. *"Shawn? Talk to me, love, please."*

Still nothing, although he did blink a couple of times.

Something niggled in the back of her mind. Earlier, when she had been by her mother's bedside, he had tried to offer her some kind of strength, but she'd pushed him away. That was until he had curled up with her, using his cat. She looked around to see her father had already returned to his room. She knew he would have stern words for her later. She winced a little, knowing that wasn't going to be a fun conversation. She started taking her clothes off, then gave her cat full rein.

I take over. I curl up with him this time, her cat said.

One of us has to reach him or his beast.

Watching through her cat's eyes, Belle saw her feline wrap around Shawn's legs. She moved around in circles a couple of times before she sat in front of her mate and began licking his hand. She could taste the salt from his sweat. She moved again, going to his other hand and doing the same. Gradually the scent of his fear and pain began to recede. Belle sighed mentally, so pleased her cat was breaking through his walls. As Shawn began to move his fingers, entwining them along and in her fur, she sent her cat a flow of warmth.

I speak to my mate. He says he passes strength to yours. He no happy with you.

Pffft, I'm not happy with me. It was something so bloody

simple and yet so devastating for him.

Shawn lowered his body to the floor and curled up against Belle's cat.

"I'm sorry, Belle." His voice came out hoarse, as if he was trying to talk around a lump in his throat. "I don't know what happened. When you started shouting I was transported back to when Rosie would start. I don't mean to put you in her shoes. Babe, I'm so sorry."

She could feel his tears falling on her cat's pelt. He sobbed gently against her until she couldn't take his pain any longer. She wanted to wrap her arms around him. Pulling her other half back, she shifted until she lay against Shawn as naked as the day she was born.

"It's not your fault," she said, caressing his damp cheek, his head resting against her breasts. "If anything, it was mine. I should have thought…remembered. I'm sorry, my mate." She wrapped her arms around his neck and placed her nose against his pulse to feel it racing. "Hold me, Shawn. Wrap your arms around me and let me love you."

He did as she asked, leaving them both sitting in her parents' kitchen, curled around each other tightly.

"Belle."

She looked up from her mate's neck to see her father. He must have come back into the room when all was quiet. Shit! She'd missed that again. *Bloody good enforcer I make.* But then embarrassment again swept through her; what else were her parents going to see and hear today?

"Don't bother with thinking, girl," her father warned, shaking his head. "We will talk later when all is settled. Now go get dressed and take your mate home. You two need to talk."

"Okay, Pop," she replied, then gasped when Shawn suddenly stood and lifted her in the air, his arms and hands hiding bits of her she knew her father didn't wish to see.

With her arms wrapped around Shawn's neck, he carried her to her bedroom. She dressed silently, then begin packing a small backpack to take to Shawn's. She didn't agree with her father about moving out, but she wouldn't disobey him either.

As she moved around her room, Shawn sat on the end of her bed, watching her quietly. The air seemed thick with things they needed to talk about, but she knew this wasn't the time. Her mind kept going in circles with what had happened to the point she growled low at herself while mentally telling her brain to shut the fuck up.

Zipping the bag, she held out her hand for Shawn to take, and was glad when he did. Taking one last look at her room, as if to say goodbye, she walked down the hallway to her parents' room. Knocking softly, she waited for permission to enter.

"Come in," her father said gruffly.

She opened the door. "I'm off now," she said with tears burning behind her eyes.

Her mother lay in bed, propped up with many pillows, and her father sat at her side, his feet on the floor.

"Come here, love." Her mother held her arms out to her.

Belle dropped her bag and Shawn's hand and ran into her mother's arms.

"There, there, you silly girl," her mother cooed. "You have a mate now, sweetheart. It's where you're supposed to be. We aren't far, and you can come see us every day."

Belle lifted her head from her mother's chest, and her mother wiped away the tears on her cheeks. "I love you, Mum."

"Aw, sweetheart, I love you more." With a kiss to her forehead, her mother released her. "See you tomorrow, okay?"

Belle nodded. She placed a kiss on her father's cheek and walked from the room. Shawn had her bag in his hand, and this time he held his hand out to her. She grabbed it and entwined her fingers around his.

"Another chapter in my book, right?" she asked Shawn.

"Our chapter." He smiled, placing an arm around her shoulder.

* * * *

Shawn couldn't believe he had freaked as badly as he had. He was in the kitchen making a pot of tea while Belle unpacked her bag. He was still shaking inside.

At least you aren't calling yourself all those bad names, his tiger reminded him.

Only because you got pissed off and swiped my insides.

You no idiot. Just remember bad things.

How long is it going to take me to not go there, to not freak over a raised voice or hand? How long 'til the damage I let Rosie do stops affecting me? Shawn sighed heavily, the steam from the boiling kettle billowing outward as he blew through it.

Talk to mate. She feel bad too. His tiger shook his head. *Humans think too much. I mate female, get her mind off other things.*

Shawn actually smiled at that. Such a primitive thought, and yet he remembered how his tiger had calmed his female when Belle was pissed. *It might work with you, buddy, but alas, we humans need to talk things through.*

Sex first, talk after. Calmer, his tiger grumbled, trying to get his point across.

Shawn sent his feline a flow of warm, loving energy. He knew that he and Belle had to talk. He had to explain where he had gone mentally when she'd started shouting.

The one thing that had shocked him though was Barry telling his daughter to stay with her mate. He imagined that with his partner dying, Barry would want his daughter beside him. What would he do if, God forbid, anything ever happened to Belle and they had kits? Shaking his head, he stopped that thought before it went further. He didn't want to think of anything happening to Belle.

He'd just put the top on the teapot when Belle walked into the kitchen. Grabbing two mugs, he placed them on a tray and carried it over to the table.

"All unpacked?" he asked.

"Yeah. Well, I suppose where we live has been sorted," she said with a chuckle. Her cheeks had a hue of red to them. She seemed awkward, like she was afraid of saying the wrong thing.

Shawn sat down in one of the oak chairs that matched the table and pulled his mate onto his lap. Her arms automatically wrapped around his neck. Leaning toward her, he kissed her bow-shaped lips. One kiss wasn't enough, and he pecked, nibbled, and tasted hers lips.

"We need to talk, big man," she said, pushing against his chest before the kiss could become any more heated.

"I know, but a little distraction helps, right?" he asked, knowing he had a cheeky smile on his face.

Chapter 16

Shawn and Belle sat at the kitchen table talking for the next few hours. He began telling her how it all started with Rosie and how when she'd gotten the job as manager her moods became worse. He never knew who he would find when he got up or came home from work—Nice Rosie or Bitchy Rosie. By the end of the relationship her moods had grown worse to the point that Bitchy Rosie was much more prevalent.

"When you started shouting earlier, I had a major flashback. It was so real. It was if I was standing in the room with Rosie. I could smell her perfume, hear her screeching voice yelling at me. I froze, waiting for whatever you chose to hit me with. I couldn't distinguish what was you and here—it all blurred together. I'm sorry."

Belle was still sitting in his lap, which made him feel worse for telling her that. He hated he'd gone to a place where Belle and Rosie were the same. A part of him wanted to put her on her own chair so she wasn't touching him, and at the same time another part of him wanted to pull her closer and hold her tight.

"Hey." Belle's palm stroked his cheek. He looked up, seeking her eyes. "It's okay. I know it's going to take us time to learn things about each other, and this just throws a few fences in the way for us to jump over. It's the shifter way, we're mates. We can do this together." She sounded so sure. Her eyes told him there was truth in her words.

He closed his eyes briefly. "It's that simple to you? I'm scared my problems will drive a wedge between us. I can't help it when it happens."

"Together, okay? We can make a pact. I work on my temper and not ranting when I see red about things and talk to you first. And you work on letting me know what drags you back to the past so we can either work with it or dodge it 'til it doesn't happen anymore."

"You know what my tiger suggested?" He grinned, his cock already hardening under her butt.

"Mmm, I wonder," she said, copying his smirk, and wriggled.

He covered her mouth with his, slipping his tongue inside when her lips parted for him. "I love the taste of you," he murmured.

"And I you," she whispered back, then nibbled on his ear. His cock was now full-blown erect to a painful point. "Move your hands to the arms of the chair."

He lowered his hands from around her slowly so she could place her feet on the floor. Once she was steady he did as she asked. She moved over to his CD player and turned it on. Justin Timberlake's *Can't Stop the Feeling* sounded through the mini-speakers, filling the room.

She turned her back to him, looking over her shoulder, her face lit up with a sexy smile. She began to sway her hips, then the rest of her body moved to the music. She circled her hips while her hands roamed over her shirt. Her seductive dance had her turning in circles. He could see her nipples sticking out through her clothes. He breathed deeply and caught the scent of her growing arousal. Her fingers edged around the hem of her top and she pulled it up, all the while keeping to the beat of the music.

His cock jerked against the zipper of his jeans. His fingers embedded into the arm of the chair. Her top went flying somewhere across the room, but he didn't follow it, because his gaze was firmly settled on his mate, her tanned skin rippling and moving as she continued her dance. She turned away from him, her hands dipping low, somewhere he couldn't see. She must have undone the button of her jeans, because she began to shimmy and they dropped slowly down to her knees. She looked over her shoulder, her smile still bright and sexy. His eyes flickered to her lips when she ran her tongue along them. He groaned, his hands tightening around the arm of the chair, making it creak.

Stepping out of her jeans, she scooted them across the floor with her foot. She danced a little more in front of him in just her lacy underwear. Her hands lifted up to her hair, where she ran her fingers through the short spikes. She twirled until she again had her back to him. This time he watched one of her fingers shift into a single claw, and she lifted it to the back of her bra strap and flicked it until it snapped in half. With a shake of her shoulders, her bra fell down her arms and onto the floor.

He was captivated. She twisted around, her hands dancing in the air above her head. It gave him an eyeful of her wonderful, luscious breasts bouncing around, her perky nipples pointing directly at him. His mouth watered as he imagined enveloping them.

"Like what you see, big boy?"

His gaze flicked back up to her eyes to see them sparkling. Unable to speak, he just swallowed and nodded. He felt like a teen getting his first look at a naked woman.

She carried on swaying, flicking her hips back and forth. She turned and spun in a circle, sticking her arse out at him. How much more could he take? She moved closer to him, her hands gliding over her skin, across her breasts with a quick nipple pinch, then stroking her stomach. Down to her white, lacy panties. She shifted both forefingers to claws and slid them into the sides of the thin material and tugged, leaving the material to flutter to the floor.

She dropped to her knees and twisted, then crawled toward him until her hot, little mouth was an inch from his crotch. He was so tempted to move his hands, run them through her hair, or unzip his pants and let his shaft spring clear of its confinement. He didn't have to wait long, Belle cupped his knees, her fingers spreading over his thighs as they moved up toward his groin. With a quick look up she lowered her mouth and licked up the crease of his jeans. A shiver went through him. Her fingers found his zipper and she began pulling it down, ever so slowly. He had to close his eyes and breathe deeply before he came in his pants.

How long since she'd started this dance? It felt like forever. His breathing picked up, and his heart started to race. His button flicked open with a ping and he felt the warm breath of her mouth over the tip of his cock. He had to grit his teeth when her tongue followed.

"You are going to be the death of me," he ground out.

"A good way to go though." She chuckled, her hands enclosing around his member, pulling it out of his jeans.

A moment later her mouth enveloped his erection. A hissed gasp broke from his throat. The vibration of her moan rippled through his cock. If he didn't take control soon, he was going to spill his seed down her throat, which wasn't a bad loss, he just wanted to be inside Belle when he did. Slowly, she began bobbing, her tongue sliding up the large vein and swiping just under the mushroomed head. His hips undulated unconsciously, which thrust his sex to the back of her throat. She swallowed. His eyes closed and he called her name. She moaned again.

A crack sounded, and he looked down to see the broken arms of the chair in his hands. Her mouth left his cock, and she began to laugh. With a shake of his head, he dropped the pieces of wood and stood. His clothes were quickly deposited on the floor, and he grabbed his mate around her waist, lifting her up against his body, his hands holding her firmly under her butt. Her legs wrapped around his waist. The music changed to Shakira's *Try Everything* as he carried her to their room and dropped her onto the bed.

"You had your fun, sweetheart. My turn now." He grinned at her as he covered her body with his.

He took her mouth, tasting himself. Their tongues entwined and danced. Then slowly he made his way down her body, sucking her breasts into his mouth as he'd wanted to earlier. After each nipple was swollen he moved down over her stomach, dipping his tongue into her belly button and making her squirm. He ran his tongue over the tiny dark blonde strip that covered her nether lips, until finally he reached his goal. Her honey pot. He lapped, nipped, and suckled until her legs shook. He glided his teeth over her tiny nub and thrust a finger deep inside her core. A satisfied purr sounded from his chest as his mate screamed his name into the air, her pussy tightening around his fingers as she came.

* * * *

Belle's arms were limp noodles. Her heart raced from her orgasm, and satisfaction thrummed through her. Her man sure knew how to go down on a woman. It would only ever be her he tasted now; he was hers, and she was his.

She raised her head slightly to look down at him. He was crawling up her body, his mouth wet from her juices. Wiping his face on the inside of his upper arm, he hovered over her, smiling from ear to ear.

"Mmm, you taste like a fine wine." He kissed her, delving his tongue between her lips, letting her taste herself combined with his.

He pulled back and lifted her legs up and over his shoulders, then shuffled forward so his cock lined up with her pussy. Shifting a touch more, the head of his cock entered her. She raised her hands so her fingers entwined in his thick mop of brown hair and pulled him down to gain access to his lips again.

He thrust deep, their combined juices making it easy. She gasped into his mouth. He pulled back only to surge back in. It felt deeper to take him this way. He began the frantic race to the end. In and out. Fast and hard. His movements becoming jerky the more excited he became.

His stomach rubbed against the back of her thighs, their skin dampened with perspiration. The sexy sounds of skin slapping against skin filled the room. Low grunts and moans joining them. He moved his arm from beside her head, and his hand roamed down over her skin and in between them until he found that tiny bundle of nerves that turned her to goo. With a rub of his fingers, she rocked and came around his cock, taking him with her. He roared into the air while she screamed out his name.

Eventually he softened enough to slide from her pussy, their combined juices slipping out too. He rolled, allowing her legs to lower, then pulled her over his chest. She could feel his thumping heart beat slow as they rested.

"No regrets, right?" he asked, bringing her out of her relaxed stupor.

"Huh?" She lifted her head to look at him. He looked worried.

"I suppose I'm still uneasy in case I'm not what you want."

She slapped his chest slightly and lowered her head back over his heart. "Shut up and go to sleep. You are mine, and I am yours. Can't change our minds now even if we wanted to."

She felt him release a breath he'd been holding, and she smiled. Closing her eyes, she relaxed into sleep.

Chapter 17

The sound of raindrops pinging against the window woke
Shawn from the best night's sleep he'd had in ages…well, between
the times either he woke Belle up to fuck her or she woke him up
with her mouth sucking his cock. For the first time in what seemed
forever Shawn felt relaxed and comfortable. He didn't feel like he
was on edge, waiting for the woman in his life to bite his head off.

He curled up closer to Belle, shoving his morning erection
firmly between her butt cheeks with confidence she would
reciprocate rather than push him away. He buried his nose into her
neck and breathed deeply…wild daisies and honey mixed in with the
scent of the sun and sex. He licked over his mark on her neck, and
she shivered and stirred. He continued nibbling along her neck until
she moaned and one of her hands shot to the back of her and
wrapped around his shaft.

"Morning, my tigress."

She turned on her back, ungrasped his cock, and stretched,
her perky tits reaching for the ceiling as she did. He lowered his head
and sucked the one closest to him, rolling it around in his mouth.

"Didn't you get enough last night?" she teased.

He released her nipple with a pop and smiled down at her.
"Nope. Never enough." He leaned over and sucked her other nipple
into his mouth.

"Mmm, so good," she murmured, twisting to lay on her side.
"What time is it?" She stretched to look over his shoulder at the

alarm clock on the bedside table. "Bugger," she swore, throwing herself back on the bed with a frown. "Monday morning and back to normal." She sighed.

"Bloody hell, has it really been a week?" he asked before checking the time himself. 6:56. Damn. The honeymoon week Harris had given to Belle as a gift, so to speak, had sped past.

Good to her word, Belle had visited her parents every day as well as spending an hour with Felix. The rest of the time, the pair of them had begun to get to know each other, in more ways than one. Shawn had finally been able to relax and get into the swing of having a normal relationship. He felt as if everything was right in his world for once. He'd had a few flashbacks, but otherwise he'd managed them to the point where he wasn't too upset by them.

With Belle at his side, he'd also managed to do quite a lot of meet-and-greet around the village. His favorite couple were actually the oldest pair. May and Fred had both been born in the village, their parents too. They shared their own stories, and also included a few of the other townspeople's stories too. They told Shawn all about how the village had grown, the Alpha's keeping them safe, and the peace they maintained. They also had a story to share about Belle, much to her embarrassment.

There was one thing though that marred his happiness— Rosie. The police hadn't been in contact with him, Harris, or Garrett. *That has to be good, right?* But as time went on, a shadow still followed him. He wished it was all over and he could just get on with his life.

Belle nudged him, bringing him out of his thoughts. "Hey there, you okay?"

"Yeah, just wondering why the police haven't been in contact."

"What comes will come, we will get through it. Now…how about putting that," she said, pointing toward his erection, "to good use with a quickie in the shower before we both have to get to work."

Shawn smiled as his mate quickly climbed out of bed and danced toward the bathroom, waggling her booty as she went.

* * * *

The village surgery wasn't very large, one of the main reasons being that shifters were rarely ill. Ben, however, covered a large array of things, such as also being the village psychiatrist.

"Morning, Frankie," Shawn greeted a bobcat shifter as he entered the reception. "I'll let Ben know that you've arrived."

Shawn didn't know the man's background, only that he was one of two bobcats in the community. However, he did know that Frankie was nearing his forties and was seeing the doc to help with his depression. Desolation was the main illness among shifters. The animal side seemed to hit a point where all it wanted to do was push the human side to mate, have kits and a family. About half of Stonesdale's residences had reasons to not leave the village, which meant a lot of them didn't find their mates and settled for imprinting, but alas, some didn't want to just settle. This, of course, led to a few getting depressed.

Picking up the phone, Shawn pressed the button for Ben's office and informed him that Frankie was there.

"Send him through please, Shawn."

"Frankie, Ben will see you now."

"Thanks."

"*Shawn?*" Harris's voice sounded inside Shawn's mind.

"*Yes, Alpha?*"

"*Are you busy?*"

"*Ben has no more patients to see today. Not sure if he has anything else planned.*"

"*I'll take care of Ben. I need you to come to the police station please.*"

"*Umm, okay.*"

Dread clenched at Shawn's heart. He couldn't tell what kind of mood Harris was in, his speech had basically been monotone. Was this where his life would change for the better or worse?

His thoughts then went to Belle. Being an enforcer, she would know if any visiting police were around. Should he contact her or not? Deciding not to, he stood, tidied up, and then gathered his jacket. He glanced around, wondering if this was the last time he would see the surgery. *I hope not.* He sighed.

Walking the few feet next door to the police station, his emotions and thoughts weighed heavily. His question was answered about a visitor when he saw a black SUV parked outside. Belle had to know they were there.

With his hand on the door handle, he paused and breathed

deeply, closing his eyes as a wave of nausea rolled over him. Shit, what if they decided he was guilty? Could he hack prison if it came to that?

No! He had to think positive. He was innocent. Lifting his chin, he pushed the handle down and walked into the small police station. Scents of two different males hit him as well as his Alpha and the local police officer.

Harris strode toward him, a grim look on his face, which caused the nausea Shawn felt to hit the back of his throat. Swallowing profusely to keep from throwing up, he waited to hear what the man had to say.

"Don't worry, son," Harris said, placing a hand on his shoulder and giving him a gentle squeeze. "I think they're here for good, not bad. That detective that came before, Johnathon Canker, sure has a face on him. Looks like he has a skunk under his nose."

Shawn nodded. "Here's hoping." He let out a breath and received another squeeze before Harris turned and walked down the hallway with Shawn following him.

"Ah, Mr. Burr," Garrett greeted him when they entered his office. Shawn nodded his acknowledgement. "Our visitors have some news. Please take a seat." He gestured to the one remaining leather chair opposite his desk.

Sitting down, Shawn looked around. Johnathon Canker was sitting to his left, while on his right sat Detective Harry Small, who'd come last time as well. Harris was right about Canker, he looked like he'd swallowed a bitter pill.

"Detective Small has some news for you." Garrett smiled at Shawn.

Shawn turned his head to the neatly dressed bloke wearing a dark blue suit.

"We do indeed. First, we would like to extend our apologies for the way you were treated last time we were spoke." The detective turned his head to Canker whose expression darkened into a scowl. "Upon our departure here we went back and interviewed Miss O'Hare again. The reason it has taken us so long to get back to you is we were trying to follow up with some other witnesses, especially the neighbor who called the emergency services on the night you were stabbed. We found a few holes in your fiancée's story—"

"Ex," Shawn interrupted the man. He didn't want Rosie to be anything of his anymore.

"Yes, sorry. As I was saying, there were a few holes in Miss O'Hare's statement. When she was interviewed at the hospital, she accused you of inflicting her injuries. But your neighbor said she left the house perfectly well, except for the blood on her hands and clothes. Plus, we also spoke with another neighbor who witnessed the same thing. That person also told us that…" The detective shuffled a few pieces of paper from a file he had in his hand. "*Miss O'Hare frequently raised her voice, screaming all kinds of profanities at her partner*…you. Anyway, Mr. Burr, we came today first to apologize for the way you were treated last time. And second, sir, being you *are* the victim we came to let you know, in person, that because of the evidence we have gathered, there is a warrant out for your fi…" The copper quickly cleared his throat to cover his near mistake. "Your ex-fiancée. However, when we showed up to arrest her, we discovered that she had disappeared, along with two of her brothers. Her other siblings were interviewed, but I'm afraid weren't helpful in locating her whereabouts. This leaves us with a difficult situation. We aren't able to do much else until we have Miss O'Hare in custody. The only other advice I…we…" He gestured to his fellow officer. "…can offer you is that maybe you could apply for a restraining order."

Shawn nearly snorted at the thought of a restraining order. It wouldn't do shit. It was a piece of paper that neither Rosie nor her brothers would pay the slightest notice to. Shawn's friend and boss Paul had also suggested that after encouraging Shawn to leave Rosie. But he too said, knowing what Rosie and her brothers were like, it wouldn't be worth the paper it was written on.

"They don't know where I am, right?" Shawn asked, feeling hopeful.

"No, sir, I don't think they have any idea."

"Good," Shawn breathed out a sigh of relief. "I will think about the restraining order. Thank you," he said, forgetting for a second he was in a village protected by shifters. He almost slapped himself when he remembered.

He stood, ready to leave the room and go find his mate. At least now he felt he would finally get some justice rather than recrimination. He held his hand out to the detective, who took it and smiled while shaking it.

"Good luck, Mr. Burr, and again, I give you our apologies."

Shawn then offered his hand to Johnathon Canker. "Bygones be bygones as far as I'm concerned," Shawn said with a smile.

The detective stood and shook his hand, albeit rather limply and with his lips turned up as if he smelled something bad. Shawn shrugged and turned his back to him, then walked out of Garrett's office with Harris close behind.

Chapter 18

Stepping outside, a body Shawn hadn't had time to see, spot, or smell dived straight into him, knocking him back a step. As legs wrapped around his waist and the smell of his female hit his nostrils, his hands found her backside and held on.

"Harris told me. Oh my God, I'm so happy for you. I still want to kick that detective's backside from here to kingdom come though," Belle said in between smothering kisses over his face.

Harris boomed out a laugh beside him.

"Get down, you limpet." Shawn chuckled.

She stopped kissing him and pulled back to look at his face. "See, I told you they would believe you." She lowered her legs to stand in front of him, her head resting on his chest, her arms wrapped around his waist.

The air never seemed so fresh as it did then. He'd walked into the police station like a dead man walking, but he'd come out not only a free man but one that was believed. He hadn't realized just how much this—the knowledge that the police honestly thought he was the one who'd been the abuser—had been laying on him like a lead coat.

"Go home, the pair of you," Harris ordered with a smile.

Shawn didn't think twice. Entwining his fingers in his mate's hand, he proudly walked home with her beside him. He was free and, most importantly, believed.

Mate always believed you. That's more important than

human police.

I know, but still, it's a relief to finally know that I won't be facing some kind of assault charge.

Mate know truth, his tiger repeated.

Shawn couldn't deny that at first Belle had believed he'd been the abuser rather than the victim, but after a chat with Harris she came to trust that Shawn couldn't hurt any female. It had been one of the first things she'd spoken to him about.

The black SUV carrying the two officers drove past them. Shawn was glad to see them go, but pleased with the news they had brought.

Time to play? his cat asked with a smirk.

Shawn quietly agreed as they reached their front door. Plucking the key out of his pocket, he inserted it into the lock and opened the door. Taking a step inside, Shawn pulled his mate into his arms.

"I love you." The words slipped out of his mouth, he hadn't even thought about saying them. It shocked him, but only for a second before he repeated the three simple words, with everything he felt for her inside of him. "I love you more than I ever thought I could love another."

"I love you too, my tiger."

Shawn could feel the love she inserted into the same words he'd just told her. He lowered his head and kissed her lips. His cock was rigid in his pants, jerking, eager to get out.

"You know, now that I'm a free man it means you have to

put up with me, don't you?" He nuzzled his mouth just under her ear, a place he knew made her shiver.

"I don't *put up with you*," she said, pulling back and looking at him with serious eyes. "I want you." Her hands reached for his belt, and with quick dexterity, she had it undone in seconds. "I need you." Next, she undid the button on his black work pants. "You are mine."

He gasped when her hand reached down and grasped his hardness and began pumping it. His hips undulated along with her movement.

"My heart belongs to you, no matter where you are, get me?" she said.

He picked his mate up, slinging her over his shoulder, and carted her to their bedroom. Kicking the door shut, he dropped Belle on her feet and ordered her to strip.

"Maybe I don't want to." She placed her hands on her hips, her forehead creating a crease between her eyes when she frowned.

Oh fuck. He froze. Had he gone too far? He'd been in the moment and given her an order. Memories flashed. Was she angry? Was she about to scream at him? His heart began to thud in his chest as fear gripped him. *Think, man, think!*

She's playing. Scent her, his tiger quickly told him.

He lifted his head and scented the room. His heart began to slow. He smelled her arousal, joy, and Belle all tied together. No hint of anger at all. He studied her body language. Although she had her hands on her hips, her posterior was tilted in a playful manner. Her breasts were pushed out, her nipples tight and hard, pushing through the material of her top and bra. Glancing at her face, he saw her lips were slightly lifted at the corners. He knew he took his time to stare, but Belle's attitude was passive, as if she knew he needed to work things out in his mind. He didn't miss the quick raise of her eyebrows, a silent question—was he ready? His tiger was right, she wanted to play.

He relaxed, took a breath, and pulled himself back out of the past. If she wanted to play, he could do that.

"Then perhaps I need to help you…want." He pulled his belt slowly from the loops of his trousers and folded it in half. He snapped it, a crack sounding around the room.

"Oh no," Belle pretended to shriek. "Are you going to use that on me?" She placed her hands over her mouth. Shawn caught a swift glimpse of a smile.

"Are you going to be a good girl?" He snapped the belt again.

Belle grabbed the hem of her top, then slowly pulled it over her head, revealing her silky, tanned skin, and dropped it onto the floor. He knew what it was like to taste the sun on her skin, to lick it all over.

"I could be a good girl, sir. But perhaps I need a little incentive."

"Then take the rest of your clothes off," he ordered, this time lowering his voice so it came out a deep rumble.

Belle undid the button of her jeans and shimmied so they

lowered around her ankles. Knowing she was going to bend to untie her trainers and take them off, he halted her.

"Stop! Turn around first, then bend over. I want to see your backside in the air."

She did as he bid. Her arse swayed in the air as she undid the laces of her trainers and pulled them off, followed by her socks, and stepped out of her jeans. He walked up close behind her, her backside resting against his hard shaft. He dropped the belt and cupped her buttocks through the lace of her panties. He wanted skin against skin. He pulled each side of the thin material until they snapped and fluttered to the floor.

He squeezed the bare skin of her buttocks and molded them in his palms. For the first time in his life he wanted to bring a hand back and slap one of the globes until it left a handprint. It wasn't abuse, right?

As if reading his mind, Belle looked over her shoulder at him and urged, "Do it."

His dick jerked again. Could he? Should he? His hands shook slightly as they rested on her butt.

"Do it!" she ordered.

Without another thought he lifted his right hand and brought it down on her buttock. A resounding slap of skin-on-skin filled the air. It excited him to see a red handprint appear on her skin. Guilt came next. He'd marked her, and he'd become excited about it.

Belle stood, turned, and wrapped her arms around his neck. Lavender eyes stared back at him. "It wasn't wrong. You didn't hit me out of anger. It was sexual."

"But I hit you." Nausea crept up and lodged in his throat. He looked down, not wanting to meet her eyes.

"I wanted you to do it. I want you to do it again, but only if you want to." She paused. "Did you want to do it?" she asked, lowering her head and looking up so she could meet his eyes.

He frowned and looked down even more, not wanting to meet her eyes.

"Did you?" she asked again.

"Yes."

"Did you enjoy it?"

Oh God, had he! "Yes, briefly."

"Look at me, my tiger."

He lifted his head and looked into her eyes. He didn't see hate, he saw lust and love.

"I liked it. I want you to do it again. It makes me hot. Scent me. Let my body tell you the truth." She kissed his cheek. "Close your eyes and breathe."

She sucked on his bottom lip, and he closed his eyes and breathed. Her arms released his neck and slid to the top of his shoulders, then down his arms. Her fingers entwined around his for a few moments before she dropped her hands to his sides. With his eyes closed he couldn't see what she was doing, but he felt her twist in front of him and her butt rested against his groin. He moved his hands and found the side of her thighs. Moving them up, he ran them over her silky skin until he knew he rested on each side of her hips.

"Breathe, baby," she encouraged.

He did a couple of times, then opened his eyes. Her forearms laid on the bed, her weight being held up by them. He met her eyes looking back at him over her shoulder. She smiled, her eyes lighting up her beautiful face.

He looked down at her bare arse and saw the perfect handprint on the right cheek. His cock was rock solid, and his heart thundered in his chest. He raised his left hand this time and dropped it with a slap. Excitement rippled through him again, his breath picking up to a slight pant. He noticed Belle's had picked up too. He brought his right hand up and down, then his left. Belle groaned in pleasure, and his dick jerked. Her buttocks glowed a bright red, his handprints showed in different ways at the edges. Belle pushed her butt back at him and wriggled it.

What was so fascinating about seeing her buttocks a shade of red, or was it the fact that his hand had caused it? She was right though, he wasn't doing it out of anger, it was…sexual? He brought his hand down again on her right buttock. His cock was hard enough to hammer nails. Here she was naked in front of him and he was still dressed. Even that small thing gave him a sense of satisfaction. He felt in charge, like the alpha male he wanted to be, was that wrong?

Shaking his head, he mentally told himself to stop questioning things, himself, to just let it happen. They were two happy, consenting adults. He placed a hand between her shoulder blades and let it drift down her spine, and she shivered in response. He carried on down, past the small of her back and over her warm buttocks, which he stroked gently, feeling the heat emanating from them. Belle moaned and wriggled again.

He skimmed his hand over to her hips and down underneath her until he reached her very wet folds. Her clit wasn't hard to find; it was already swollen and firm. Pressing on it, he received another groan from Belle. His kitten wanted this.

* * * *

Each time her man brought his hand down on her backside, it stung, but only for a fraction of a second before a warm, caressing burn took over. She'd read books where the heroine loved to have her butt smacked, or even received a spanking for misbehavior. She'd often wondered what it would feel like. She never imagined it would feel as erotic as it did.

Slap! Pain, then a burn. She wriggled her butt against Shawn's erection inside his pants. She needed him inside her. She'd been the one to start this and was glad that even after the hiccup at the beginning Shawn was enjoying it too. The scent of their pheromones filled the room. Her cat was purring deep inside her. She also knew that for some reason this was giving Shawn the kind of confidence boost he needed. He didn't stutter his movements, they were relaxed and sure.

His hands roamed between her legs and one of his long fingers slipped just inside of her, making her gasp. His thumb pushed down on her clit. She couldn't help but squeeze her thighs together for some kind of friction. *Slap*! His left hand came down on her butt again. This time a small yelp left her that turned into a purr.

"My kitten likes this, does she?" he asked, his voice husky enough to give her goose bumps. "Balls deep, that's what I'm going to be real soon."

Belle whimpered. She wanted his cock deep inside her. She wanted to feel his balls slap her clit, to hear his grunts when he hit the top of her cervix.

"Please," she begged. She had never been close to desperation for anything as she felt right now.

His thumb began to move over her clit, and she didn't know if she should open her legs wider or squeeze them again. Her pussy clenched at thin air.

"Please, Shawn. Anything. Please," she pleaded, unsure what she really needed right then, she just needed something.

First, he fully inserted a finger, then he added another and began pumping away inside her. Finally, her pussy had something to try and hold onto. He began to get faster, pushing his digits as far as he could, and his thumb flicked over her clit. Oh God, she was so close.

"Yes. Yes. Yes," she chanted.

Another slap on her backside and her whole body tensed as a huge orgasm rocketed through her. Her breath stilled in her lungs until she sang out Shawn's name. Well, she more screamed it out than singing it. Her hips jerked as he fingered her until the flutters of her pussy slowed down.

Her breasts felt heavy pressing against the quilt below her. Her legs felt like jelly. If it wasn't for his hands now firmly wrapped around her waist, she was sure she'd be a puddle on the floor.

Slowly, her mate picked her up and laid her on the bed on her back, her legs hanging off the side of it. She looked at her man through half-lidded eyes and smiled at him. His eyes were like the tropical, clear blue seas she'd seen in books. He looked happy and relaxed, more so now than she'd ever seen him. He opened her legs enough to move in between them.

Was it wrong that she felt a little kinky and a little venerable with him still being fully clothed while she was naked? He loomed over her until he placed his weight on his arms either side of her shoulders.

"You like that, my naughty little kitten?" he asked.

She felt too sated to answer so just hummed while biting on her bottom lip. His gaze flicked down to them and he licked his own. In a flash, his lips were on hers. He kissed her like a man who was desperate and needy.

His erection still hidden inside his pants rubbed against her groin. She moved her hands lower to the top of his trousers, blindly seeking the button to release it. Shawn's hand grasped her wrist, and he moved position so he knelt between her legs. Her gaze flicked from his face to his hands that were releasing the button on his trousers. *Finally!*

He had a sexy smile on his face. She tilted her head up to watch him lower the zipper, and she was surprised to see he'd gone commando to work. She hissed in a breath when he pulled his long, thick erection out. A pearly drop of pre-cum at the top had her licking her lips.

Chapter 19

Belle pushed herself up onto her elbows, but Shawn shook his head. "Not this time, kitten, I'm too close."

She lowered back down. Shawn grasped his cock and pumped it up and down slowly. For a brief moment his eyes closed and he breathed deep, and another drop of pre-cum joined the first. Then his lips curled up at the edges and he dropped down on her. Her breasts pressed against his chest, her legs wrapping around his waist instantly.

With a jerk of his hips, his sex entered her, and with a second jerk he thrust deep inside her. Combined groans could be heard. Heat rushed through her cheeks and her body tingled as her pussy stretched to his fullness. She pressed her feet down on the top of his arse, silently begging him to move.

Shawn began nibbling on her neck in between whispering dirty words in her ear. His body consumed her, and she loved it. Small grunts and groans filled the room. Skin slapping against skin, with the occasional squelchy noises.

"Shaaaawwwwn," she cried out. The orgasm hit her fast; she hadn't realized she was so close.

Shawn began moving faster, even as her pussy clamped down hard around his cock. She met him thrust for thrust until finally he hissed in air and then let out a long, low, growling rumble as his body stiffened. She could feel the swell of his cock as it began jerking inside her. His body lay over the top of hers, not in a suffocating manner, but just enough that she welcomed his heat and heaviness. She could feel the beating of his heart. She wrapped her arms around his neck and pampered him with kisses while her own heart slowed.

After curling up to each other for a while, Shawn suggested they go see her parents, which she loved him more for. It was nice having a partner who knew what she needed. Her mother was sick and she didn't want a day to go past where she didn't see her.

Half an hour later they were walking through the village, heading to her parents' house.

"Thank you," she said.

"What for?" he asked, taking hold of her hand.

"For thinking of my parents as well as me."

"They are a part of me now too, aren't they?"

"Yes. Yes, they are." She nodded. "Doesn't it make missing your parents worse, having a kind of new set around?"

"In a way, but then in another way no. I miss my parents, but it's been so long since they died that it doesn't hurt as much anymore. I still wonder daily if they'd like the man I've become, even on a day when I've done something…naughty." He blushed. "I can imagine my mother scolding me, or my father scowling or giving me his disappointed look."

Belle couldn't help but laugh at his expression. She could just see herself leaning over a young boy with Shawn's smile and eyes telling him off. *Oh good Lord, where did that come from?*

Her tigress perked up. *Deep inside, you want kits.*

Not ready yet, she argued.

You fertile, young, and have mate. It going to happen. Mate and I want kits.

Belle became lost in her thoughts. Kits…now? Was she ready? Her mother was sick, and she was taking over as beta for a while. What if Shawn didn't want kits? She hadn't even thought to ask.

"Shawn?" she said hesitantly.

"Yeah?"

"What do you think about kits?"

"They are small, excitable on chocolate, and moody when you say no." He chuckled.

"Ha-ha. Seriously, would you want some, one day?"

"If you do," he replied, dodging the answer if *he* wanted some.

She stopped and stood in front of him, looking up into his crystal blue eyes. "Okay, let me rephrase that—do *you* want kits?

"With you, yes. I want a kit that looks like you, that has your attitude about life. Between us, I think we have big enough hearts that we could handle…say about, mmm…seven or eight kits."

"What?"

Shawn let out a loud belly laugh, then bent down and kissed her lovingly. "How many kits do you want?" he asked with a serious look on his face suddenly.

"Let's start with one and work from there, huh?"

Shawn smiled. "And when will that be being we aren't using

any protection?"

"Sooner than we thought? Maybe? We will handle what fate throws at us." Belle wasn't thinking just about a kit when she said that, she was also thinking about her mother and her illness. How long did she have left, and if Belle were to have a kit, would her mother get to see it?

Walking into her parents' house was definitely like coming home after a long day. The scents of the house brought the cozy feeling she loved.

"Pop?" she called out, pushing the front door closed. No answer. "Mum?" Still nothing.

That was weird. Her mother hadn't left the house in almost a month now, except to go into the back garden, and if she'd called out from there they would have heard her. *Shifter hearing.*

Belle walked down the hallway, Shawn following close behind her. "Mom. Pop?" she shouted again. Still nothing.

Fear began creeping in now. Where were her parents? Finding no one in the house, Belle was feeling frantic by the time she hit the back door. It was opened, which wasn't unusual since many in the community didn't bother locking their doors as this was probably one of the safest villages around. It wasn't shifters just trusting each other, the fact that the community had its own security helped.

Stepping outside, the breath she had been holding blasted from her lungs. Both of her parents were in the garden in their tiger forms. Each of them asleep and curled up to each other, they didn't even move or stir. A strange scent filled the air. She knew that aroma. Shaking her head, she decided to ignore it.

A small tear escaped and trickled down her cheek. She could automatically tell which tiger belonged to her mother. The poor thing looked emaciated and fragile. Its fur that had been so fine and luxurious was now tatty and even missing in places. She now knew just how ill it was.

Belle quickly turned, pushing Shawn back into the house. He tried to push back at her, a question on his lips, but she placed her finger on his lips, not letting him speak. She didn't want to intrude on her parents. It seemed like a private moment between them. Almost like they were saying goodbye to each other? No, she didn't want to think that now.

She walked back into the kitchen and turned the radio on, which was a way to let her parents know she was there when they woke. She pottered around the kitchen, and decided to make a pan of soup. She clattered the cutlery and banged the pots, basically making a lot of noise.

She paused, a laugh escaping. It wasn't a normal, happy laugh; it was one very close to the hysteria she felt inside her. She'd just pushed Shawn into the house with her finger on his lips, telling him to be quiet, and yet there she was making as much noise as possible. What a screwed up situation.

Out of the corner of her eye she saw Shawn looking at her. He didn't say anything though, just watched her. Sam Smith's *Lay Me Down* came on the radio. The carrot she'd been peeling blurred as big, fat tears began falling from her eyes. Images of her parents' beasts curled up next to each other replayed in her mind, and she could see the love between them.

Even with her mother's tiger being so sick and no longer looking good, her father's beast accepted it like it was nothing. Her parents had never married in the human way. They had merely met, mated, and her mother had changed her name. As far as they were concerned, they were married, shifter style. It meant more to them than a piece of paper saying they belonged to each other. They didn't need that; they knew it in their hearts and souls, and of course, their mating scars. In fact, a lot of the elder shifters in the community shared that feeling. Belle wondered what Shawn would want to do.

Arms slipped around her waist, and the warm body of her mate settled behind her. Shawn's heat felt good against her, and she needed the comfort at the moment. He lay his head on her shoulder.

"They have a deep love for each other. They were always touching, or if one walked into the room he or she would seek the other out. They couldn't be apart for long. I'm afraid my father will die along with my mother." She hiccupped. "No." She shook her head. "I know he will." She paused, dread filling her, and she knew what she had to do. "We have to go check on them, don't we?"

She felt Shawn nod. When shifters died in their animal forms, they didn't shift back. She had kind of known in her heart what to expect when she'd walked into the garden. Being shifters, their hearing was way better than a human, and she'd walked into her parents' house and not disturbed them. It wasn't right. What had confirmed her fears was the fact she'd been pottering around in the kitchen and had music on and they still hadn't come in. The scent in the air outside had been death. She'd smelled it before.

"I don't know if I can do it," she whispered through racking sobs.

"I'm here, right beside you. I'll even go out there for you if you want."

For a second she wanted to accept his offer. But she knew if she didn't do this, it would forever play on her mind. "No, I need to do this. But I would appreciate it if you came with me."

Shawn moved from her back and stood beside her, holding his hand out. She placed the carrot and the knife she'd been holding on the chopping board and took his hand. Together they walked to the garden.

Neither tiger had moved, and deep down she knew they weren't going to. She gulped down a breath, tears falling freely. It felt hard to breathe. Taking a few more steps, she kept her eyes on the beasts' chests, searching for any breathing movements. Nothing. She was close enough now to touch them. The same scent from before hit her nose—death.

"Mom. Pop?" she squeezed out, knowing full well they weren't going to answer, and they didn't.

She fell to her knees and ran a hand over each of the beast's fur. They were still warm, but she knew now for certain, these were just empty shells her parents had used. They'd chosen to die together in their animal form.

Had they known? Why didn't they phone her? What could she have done if they had? So many questions ran through her mind. One second she was angry for them leaving her behind, the next she felt like her heart would stop from grief.

She threw back her head and howled into the air. She hadn't had a chance to say goodbye. She didn't let them know just how much they meant to her. How much she loved them. Her cat cried with her. Deep inside she howled along with Belle.

She didn't know how long she knelt with her parents, or how long she cried pain-filled tears. At some point she recognized the voices of Harris and Felix and a few others. When Shawn had tried to pick her up, she'd screamed at him, fighting to stay with her parents. She wanted them to know how much she loved them.

She smelled Ben when he came close to her, but she didn't care. Even when the prick to her upper arm made her feel drowsy she still didn't care. Too much pain. Too much grief. When Shawn picked her up again, she didn't have the strength to fight back. Her heart was breaking. She gave in to the sleep calling to her, curling up against Shawn's heated chest, and cried until she couldn't cry any longer.

Chapter 20

A week later

It was Saturday morning and Shawn had had enough. Belle had ignored him all week. She'd still been in shock, so Shawn had made arrangements with Harris for her parents' wake and funeral. The Grants had been laid to rest in the same white casket, which wasn't an unusual request for the village. The undertaker had explained that a lot of the mated pairs who were elderly often died together. They had spent so long together that even death didn't keep them apart.

After the wake, Shawn had taken Belle home where she'd fallen into a fitful sleep. The next morning when she awoke she decided it was time to go back to work. Shawn had tried to argue with her, telling her it was too soon, but Belle just ignored him and walked out the door.

That night when she had returned home, she'd refused to eat the meal he'd made, and she'd taken a shower then gone straight to bed. He kept asking himself what he'd done. What was she punishing him for? How the hell was he going to get back on her good side?

Over the week the same questions ran through him on an hourly basis, and it was making him ill. He'd even resorted to asking Ben and his Alpha for advice. Both of them had said to give her time, be patient.

It was Harris who informed him that the Grants had left their house to Belle and her mate. They wanted her to live a happy life where she grew up. They also wished that she fill it with many kits like they had hoped they'd be able to do. But yet again when Shawn had tried to talk to her she ignored him.

Shawn actually wanted her to shout at him, scream even. The silent treatment was worse than whatever Rosie had put him through. It was frustrating as hell. Even his cat was feeling it; it had apologized so many times to Shawn for leaving him when he'd been in trouble.

I always talk now. No more silence. It hurts.

They were all hurting, and Shawn had finally had enough. With permission from both Harris and Felix they'd decided to get some kind of reaction from her. During the morning's training, Felix had pushed Belle beyond her limits, hoping she would drop. She didn't. Each time she fell or was taken down by him or another enforcer, she got up and went back for more. In the afternoon Harris read her the riot act. Told her it was time to snap out of this whatever she was in. She had to face the fact that her parents were no longer around. He'd asked her if this was how her parents would want her to be. He also tried to drum in that Shawn, her mate, needed her. Her silence was killing him. But she just remained silent. Harris sent her home and told her if she didn't buck up, she wouldn't be making beta while Felix was away. Afterward he'd told Shawn everything he'd said and what had gone on during the day, then said it was up to him and he'd have his full backing for the plan Shawn had come up with.

During the day he'd boxed up all their belongings and moved them to their new house; he hoped he would get some reaction from that. And he planned to make sure that by the end of the night he had her screaming, shouting, or crying a few tears; anything just to let out the anger and tears that she'd bottled up. He wanted Belle back. The mate he'd met who had helped him heal, the mate he wanted to grow old with. This one, who was being a total stubborn bitch and bringing a lot of bad memories back, wasn't her.

As Shawn returned to his now old flat, he heard footsteps coming up the path behind him, so he ducked behind a lush bush with purple flowers. He could tell each step she made and knew which one it was, being her right trainer let the water in and it squelched slightly when it was wet. Right foot, left. Right foot, left. Then silence.

He couldn't see her from where he was hiding, but he caught her scent as the wind drifted toward him. He heard a snort, then the key being inserted into the lock. Did she know he was there? Could she scent him? He'd made sure he wasn't downwind.

He heard the click and whirl of the lock and the front door opening. He could see her now. She had paused at the threshold. She lifted her head and sniffed the air, then tilted her head as if trying to hear something. She was wearing blue jeans and a white t-shirt. He could see her bra strap through her top, and her butt looked mighty fine in her jeans. Her hair, which was normally spiked on top of her head, lay limp. She hadn't been taking care of it, or herself, this week.

"Shawn?" she called out, flicking the light switch in the hallway on and off.

He'd turned the electricity off, another point made as far as he was concerned. This was no longer home. She walked into the dim sitting room, looking around. He moved closer.

Now? his cat asked.

No, buddy. Patience.

"Shawn? I know you're here somewhere. Where's our stuff?" He watched her dart into the bedroom and come back out, and he could scent her annoyance. "Shawn," she shouted.

Now, my friend, he urged his cat.

His feline stepped into the doorway and sat down. Belle's head swung around to look at him.

"You're playing games? Now? For fuck's sake, Shawn. I'm tired. I've had a shit day. For some reason everyone saw fit to make it long and miserable. Now you?" She stomped her foot and growled low.

Shawn's cat remained where it was, and Shawn didn't say a word to her mentally either.

"Fine, you want to be like that, I'll just sleep on the bed as it is." She turned and walked back into the bedroom.

His cat stood and dived into the room after her. She was just about to throw herself on the bed when he lunged and got there first. He dug his claws into the mattress and shredded it. The material fell apart in pieces, the foam underneath it gathering in a pile for a second, and then it drifted apart, revealing the coiled springs. Shawn could feel such satisfaction from his cat as he ran his claws through the material.

Oh shit, really? he asked his beast.

She no sleep on it now. You pay Alpha.

Thanks. He snorted.

"Oh my God, you didn't just do that." Belle pointed at the bed, a slight red tinge to her cheeks. She was finally showing some kind of emotion. "Fine, you want to play that fucking game, so be it."

She turned and headed to the living area. Plopping down on the settee, she curled up into a ball, facing the back of it. *Nope, that isn't going to happen either*, he thought.

Shred the settee too? Shawn's tiger suggested.

I like your thinking.

His cat chuffed, loving the fact he was given permission to pull his claws through something else. With pleasure, it sank its claws into the back of the loveseat and shredded the brown leather. The sound of ripping and tearing filled the room. He moved around the side and repeated the action, making sure he hit the wood underneath enough to make scraping noises. Belle tossed and grumbled, but otherwise didn't react.

He moved around again until he came to the cushions underneath her body. Clamping his mouth around the foamy material, he pulled and tugged. His cat moved its head from side to side, until he managed to pull it from underneath her. Foam split from the broken seams and started scattering onto the floor.

Belle quickly stood, hand on her hips. "You're joking, right? Fucking men. Fine! I'll just ask Felix if I can stay at his place."

Shawn already knew what Felix's answer would be, because they'd spoken earlier. He waited, staring intently while Belle spoke to Felix mentally. He could tell the moment the man must have told her *no* because the frown in the middle of her forehead deepened. She turned her attention back to Shawn.

"Why? Why are you doing this? Why have you all been ganging up on me today?" She seemed to deflate for a few seconds. "I know what you're doing, I'm not stupid!" she screamed. "Tell me why."

Shawn just sat back on his haunches and stared at her.

Belle screamed again, a chest-heaving, top-of-her-lungs holler. It would seem Belle hated the silence as much as he did. "You want me to scream? If I treat you the way that fucking ex of yours did, will that get a reaction? Is that it?"

She picked up one of the shredded cushions and threw it at him. It missed him by inches. Oh, he was getting a reaction now. He felt both satisfied and guilty at the same time.

She needs this, his cat reminded him.

"Come on," she said with a long sigh. "I have had one shit day. It tops off one fucker of a week. Why are you doing this? Want me to talk? Well, screw you!"

She grabbed the other cushion and threw it at him. This one bounced off his head. His feline chuffed and still sat in the same spot.

"Don't just sit there," she yelled. The scent of her emotions now rolled off her. White hot anger.

She looked around for something else. A few ornaments sat on the fireplace, and Belle walked toward them, gathered them up, then propelled them one by one at Shawn's beast. This time his tiger reacted. He stood up, walked calmly to the front door, and outside. Shawn hoped their gamble would pay off and Belle would follow him.

He was actually pleased with himself. Not only had he instigated this fight, but when Rosie started, he tried to placard her in any way, shape, or form, which normally meant he kept his head low, his mouth shut, and curled up into a ball when the feet or fists came out to play.

"You can't just walk away now. Talk to me. Tell me why you've done this. Tell me where my stuff is." She screamed again at the top of her lungs. "Shawn!"

With his hearing so in tune with his surroundings, he heard the slight tearing of material.

Finally! Mate is coming. His tiger took off at a fast run, knowing full well his tigress was following him.

Shawn's cat ran the length of the village, running between buildings and around them. It took all his energy to keep a fair distance between them. Occasionally, when he thought she'd lost him, he would rub against something, leaving his scent behind. At some points he swore Belle's beast had caught up to him, and his cat stiffened, waiting for the pounding he would take if she landed on him. It never came. Was he sure she was still following? Yes, he knew she was. Belle was a very curious person, if she didn't follow him and find out what he was up to, it would forever bug her.

"Shawn, you fuckwad. Stop running and face me. Why have you done this? What the hell is going on?" She ranted away in his mind, a curse word inserted every few words.

He ran for near an hour until finally her ranting began to get slower and he knew she and her feline were getting tired. It was time to end this misery both she and he were suffering. He came to her parents' place and crept inside the back door, which he'd left open earlier. Reluctantly, his cat withdrew, he wanted to make sure his mate was more than tired. Shawn had to promise as soon as Belle was ready, he would let him out so he could sate his mate. *Randy bastard.*

Seeing the pair of jeans he'd left over a chair, he picked them up and quickly dressed, while keeping his eyes on the door. He caught the whiff of her scent before he saw the beautiful lavender eyes belonging to her tiger.

Chapter 21

Belle's cat sat on the back door step of her parents' house and held her head up.

"Shift and come talk to me," Shawn said gently.

The cat didn't move.

He stepped forward, hoping she'd decided not to pounce on him. Claws and bare skin didn't go together. "Shift, Belle," he ordered.

Still the feline didn't move.

He knelt down and sat just on the door's threshold opposite her. Raising a hand, he carefully moved it toward her. She flicked her ears, but let him touch the fur behind her them. He stroked her until he felt her muscles relax slightly. A gentle purring could even be heard.

"I know how you're feeling," he said. "You know about my parents. I was so numb for ages I didn't want to talk, or to face anyone. I didn't want to believe they were gone. I remember looking at their caskets and thinking they couldn't be in there. I didn't get to see their bodies, I just saw the two boxes. As silly as it sounds, in my mind, I thought they'd made the story up because they didn't want to be with me anymore."

He wrapped his arms around his knees, never taking his eyes off the cat in front of him.

"It hurts so bad it feels like someone has stabbed you in the chest, and no matter what, you can't find the knife to stop it from twisting." A lump in his throat made it hard for him to swallow. "You have to let it out, babe, or it will hurt more. You are hurting yourself. Do you think your parents would want this?"

"You have no idea what my parents would want!" Belle snapped.

"Really?" he asked. "I didn't know your parents as you did, but I can tell you now they didn't bring you up to hurt another, to hurt yourself."

Belle's cat stood and turned away.

"You run and I'll chase you," he warned. "I'm not letting you run from this any longer. I can't stand seeing you in so much pain. It's my turn to help you heal."

Angry lavender cat eyes met his. After a pause the feline shifted and Belle appeared. She turned and stood looking at the spot in the garden where they'd found her parents. Shawn had to take his eyes off her naked behind, but it was so fine his cock twitched, thinking it had been a week or more since he'd had his hands on her.

"They left me." Her voice came out a horse whisper. "They didn't even say goodbye."

Shawn rose to his feet and wrapped an arm around her waist and with the other he turned her to face him. Was it cruel of him to feel relief seeing tears on her face? He was so glad she was finally letting her grief out and talking to him.

"There could be many reasons why, I'm not going to try and justify them. But what could you have done, sweetheart? Your mother's animal was ill and dying. It is so rare I'd doubt anyone knew what to do."

Belle's head dropped onto his chest, her tears wet against his skin. "I know. I just feel so angry I didn't get to say goodbye. I'm angry 'cause they left me. I wanted my mother to see our first kit." Sobs racked Belle's body.

Shawn lifted her up and carried her inside the house and into their new bedroom. He laid her on the bed and spooned her while she cried.

"If by chance there is something on the other side of life, then I am sure we will meet them again. If there is a heaven, then they are looking down at you and smiling."

"Do you believe in a god?" she asked in a whisper.

"Everyone has different beliefs, gods, goddesses, karma. It gives everyone some kind of hope. I believe as most shifters do that fate shows us many paths, and we just chose which one to take 'til the next crossroad. Down one of the roads is our soul mate. The one that's meant to be. Some of us take the right road and find him or her, and some don't. I hope when we die, in our next life I will find you again. You are my soul mate, the one meant to be." He looked down at Belle, meeting her eyes. He meant every word he'd said. "I love you with all of my heart, now and forever." He dropped a kiss on the end of her nose.

"I'm sorry," she said after a long pause.

"Sorry?"

"Yeah, for not talking to you this week. Every time I opened my mouth, I felt angry or sad, and I couldn't speak. I just wanted to hit something."

"Well, I'm glad you didn't hit me." He chuckled. "Been there, done that."

"Hey." She turned her head to look at him. "You didn't freeze when I screamed at you. In fact…" A smile lit up her face, and even though her eyes were red-rimmed and swollen she looked beautiful. "You antagonized me more to get a reaction."

He smiled back at her and shrugged his shoulders. "I did, didn't I?" he said rather smugly.

"Weren't you afraid I'd hit you or something, like she did." He noticed she didn't say Rosie's name.

"Nah," he replied, scrunching his nose. "I know you here." He pointed to his chest. "I felt it in here, what I had to do to help you. Of course, I had to ask for help from Harris and Felix to make sure you had a bit of a bad day to make your temper rise, but…" He let the sentence trail off.

"It worked." She smiled up at him.

"Yes." He placed another kiss on her nose. "You might want to kick Felix's butt in the next training match. He said he rather enjoyed giving you a hard time."

"Oh, did he now?"

Uh-oh, should he warn Felix? *No, let the man find out for himself,* he thought, chuckling inwardly.

"Only time will heal your heart, my tigress. Let me be by your side and help you as you aided me."

Belle curled up into him and nodded. They lay there for what seemed like ages before a rumbling from her stomach had them chuckling.

"Hungry?" he asked. "Come on, let's get something to eat."

Belle looked around the room and seemed to notice all their stuff was there. "You know this is weird, right?"

"What is?"

"Well, this is our room now. My parents had sex in this room. Ugh. That is so not what I wanted to think about."

Shawn laughed so hard he had to clutch his stomach. It was the first time he'd laughed in a week. Belle looked at him and joined in. If someone was to walk in on them now, they'd think they were both nutters.

"Come on, my tigress, let me make you something to eat. Then perhaps you will let me put our stamp on the house?"

"Maybe I'll let you. But, um, not in here just yet please?" She gestured toward the room.

Shaking his head, Shawn took his mate into their new kitchen and cooked a meal.

"When are you going to tell Harris about the furniture in the old place?" she asked.

Shawn paled. Oh shit.

For the rest of the evening, Belle opened up to Shawn about how she was feeling. She kept apologizing for throwing things at him and yelling, but it was like water off a duck's back. Being shouted and screamed at by Belle didn't bother him. She wasn't Rosie.

After their meal they went through the house, placing some of her parents' things away for safe keeping. Other stuff they packed up to help some of the needy families. When it came to doing her parents' bedroom, Belle broke down crying again. This time when Shawn offered her his shirt to wipe her tears on or his body to curl up against, she accepted.

By the time the stars came out, both were so tired they fell asleep together wrapped up in each other's arms.

* * * *

Belle laid watching her mate sleep, thinking over the last week. She'd been so lost in her own black hole of anger, grief, and loss that she hadn't seen how it affected anyone else. She inwardly winced. How the hell had Shawn managed to keep his sanity? His previous fiancée had been a bitch from hell from the stories Shawn had told her. Belle sighed. She had gone and done the same thing, not with physical violence, but mental torture—silence. And yet her mate was the strongest male that she knew, besides her Alpha, of course. To have spent a week in her company after what he'd been through... He was her hero.

Last night they'd unpacked their stuff, although Shawn didn't have much, and they had also emptied her old room, spreading her personal items throughout the house. She knew they would make the house theirs over time. It just felt weird without her parents there. Sleeping in her parents' room also felt a little wrong.

She could see Shawn's morning wood tenting the bedsheet and wanted to rekindle with him, but she couldn't yet get her mind around that in her parents' bed…in their bed now. A small thump of pain hit her chest when she thought about her parents. Taking a deep breath, she swallowed it down and decided to take a shower.

As the water rained down on her, she began dreading what Harris was going to say to her. Had his warning about not being beta while Felix was away been true? Or was it just part of the plan they'd decided to put into action yesterday? She didn't know, but she was sure she'd find out later. As for Felix, she was going to kick his butt from here to kingdom come.

A cool breeze flitted over her skin as the shower door opened then closed. She scented the air and knew immediately that it was her mate.

"You didn't wake me," he stated, pressing himself against her back. His rigid erection rested just above her butt cheeks, his hands covering her breasts.

"Too creepy yet." She moved her head to the left when he started nibbling down her neck. She hissed in a breath as he firmly clamped his teeth over his mark, but not hard enough to break the skin.

"Morning, my tigress."

"Morning. You don't mind, do you?"

"Mind what?

"That I couldn't, umm…you know."

"Wake me up with your mouth around my cock." He pushed his groin further against her when he said *cock*.

Visions of doing just that had her nipples turning hard, and moisture seeped from her pussy.

He dipped his head into her neck and breathed deeply. "You like that thought, huh?"

With a hand on her shoulder, he squeezed it slightly to emphasize he wanted her to turn, and when she did, he pushed down on it, telling her without words he wanted her on her knees. She did so willingly. Looking up into his blue eyes, she stroked his erection. She could feel it grow even more rigid, and the large vein pulsed under her fingers. She licked the top, tasting the pre-cum that dribbled there, mixing with the water.

Slowly, she took his swollen member into her mouth, humming as she went. Shawn's low, erotic growl and groan mixed together as his hands entwined in her damp hair. Would it feel better if she grew her hair longer? To feel him tug on it as he pounded into her from behind. *Something to think about.*

She established a pattern, bobbing her head up and down, taking him deeper to the back of her throat each time. Shawn's hips jerked every now and again, and she could see the strain on his face as he tried to keep still. With her free hand, she cupped his balls. She molded the warm, velvet bag containing two large marble-like balls inside. Shawn jerked again, his hands gripping a bit tighter in her hair. She skimmed her teeth up his sex and heard a gasp of hissed air come from him, before she found herself being pulled up and lifted in the air. His hands gripped both of her butt cheeks, and she was virtually slammed against the white tiled wall.

Chapter 22

"What you do to me, my tigress."

Shawn's lips feasted on hers, his tongue invading her mouth. It made her all the hotter. She could feel his erection digging into her stomach only for a few moments before he picked her up a little higher.

"Help me out here," he groaned.

She knew what he meant, and she immediately slipped her hand between their bodies and found his cock. With a slight movement she had it ready at her entrance. As soon as she moved her hand, he thrust deep inside her. She shivered and both of them groaned, sharing that precious feeling they were joined to their mate.

He filled her so much she could feel his shaft swell. It didn't take long for her pussy to adjust to his fullness. Again, he nibbled, licked, and kissed her neck. She moaned when he licked over his mark. Who knew nerves ran from there all the way down to her clit? Her pussy fluttered, and that's when he moved. He lifted her higher, as easily as if she weighed no more than a feather, only to drop her back down on his sex.

Her hips undulated, and she met him thrust for thrust. Groans and sexy sounds left her throat, her cat purring away deep inside her. She wrapped her arms tighter around his neck, holding on for dear life as he pounded into her, her body moving against the wet tiles behind her. Shawn began grunting, his movements becoming jerky as they both raced toward the euphoria of a climax.

"You sexy tigress, come for me." His cock slid along her walls, moving faster with the movement of his hips.

She couldn't think; she was a wave of feelings. His thickness ramming in and out. Her feet pushed against his butt muscles, which flexed in time with his beat. His balls slapped at her arse, his head buried in her neck. His teeth raked his mark on her neck, then his fangs slipped inside her skin.

Her orgasm rocketed through her body. Her pussy clentched down on her mate's cock as the delicious sensation of her orgasm expanded out to every other single nerve in her body. Before it dissipated, she lifted her head and buried her own fangs onto his mark, claiming her mate as hers once again. He jerked one more hard, body-melting thrust, and buried himself deep inside her, his balls resting against her butt cheeks. Her pussy contracted hard enough that she could feel him jerking his seed deep into her womb.

You make kit like parents want.

It took a few moments to register what her feline had said. In her parents' will they had left her the house so she could fill it with kits like they'd wanted her to. Had she just made the beginnings of a family with Shawn? Was it the right time? Sadness then crept in; her parents should be there to see her family grow.

As long as you have them in your memories, they will always be with you. They see.

"If you believe they're looking down at you, then they are."

Belle drew her head back a little to look into Shawn's eyes. She was confused. Had she spoken to Shawn in her sexual haze instead of her cat? "W…wha… Did I say something aloud?"

Shawn chuckled and shook his head. "It would seem our cats have been chatting."

"Oh really? Now you're lying. No shifter's animal can talk to another unless they're in their form." She gestured between them. "We are still both human."

What have you been saying? she asked her cat.

Her feline chose to ignore her, just turned around in a circle in her mind and promptly fell asleep with a smug smile on her face.

"It seems our tigers have some special gift between each other."

"I've never heard of anything like this," she gasped, surprised. Her tiger still lay sleeping inside of her head, not giving her an answer. "Oh God, it means we will have no secrets at all." Belle slapped a hand to her forehead and quickly went over what she and her other half shared with each other.

Shawn chuckled. "Come on, let's get washed. We both have some explaining to do to our Alpha."

"Do we have to? Can't we delay it 'til tomorrow?"

Shawn lowered her down until her feet were firmly planted on the floor. "Nope, don't put off until tomorrow what you can do today. Plus, it's Felix's party today." He kissed her gently on the lips and started to wash them both.

"You say such wonderful, loving things to your mate in the morning," she said with full sarcasm.

After she received another light kiss, she turned the water off and they stepped out of the shower. Picking up a towel, Shawn wrapped it around her with a sexy smile. She shook her head and walked into the bedroom with Shawn following close behind.

As they both dried and dressed, Belle could feel Shawn's eyes on her. *Delaying seeing Harris wouldn't be that bad, right?* She decided to add a bit of teasing to the normal chore of dressing, and with her back toward Shawn, she dropped her towel accidently, adding an audible gasp just in case he'd looked away. She bent over to pick it up, with her legs slightly parted, knowing he would have a full view of her damp pussy. Standing straight, she grabbed hold of her panties and bent over again, giving Shawn the same view of her pussy, before skimming the thin material up her legs.

"I know what you're doing," Shawn said.

Raising an eyebrow, she turned just in time to see him trying to tuck a rather hard and huge erection into his pants. She licked her lips seductively. Lifting her arm, she ran her fingers through her hair and pushed her chest out, pretending to stretch and yawn. Shawn growled low, staring at her breasts.

"I have no idea what you mean." She smirked.

He shook his head, and then, giving her a reluctant look, he turned his back to her. "If we don't dress now, my tigress, we won't be leaving this room today."

Belle was actually tempted, but the thought of having sex in her parents'…this room was like a bucket of cold water thrown over her. She quickly finished dressing.

* * * *

After coffee and a quick breakfast, the pair went to see Harris.

"Good morning," Harris greeted them. "Belle, judging by the smile on your face it would seem your mate's plan worked."

She realized then that her crafty mate had already asked Harris for, and received, his full blessing to bring her out of her depressive hole. Belle bit the side of her mouth as a blush crept up her cheeks. *Now was not the time to mouth off.*

"Umm, there was a small problem, however," Shawn said as they sat down together in Harris's office.

"Oh, do tell," Harris said, placing his elbows on his desk and leaning on them.

"Well, Belle wasn't too pleased at the beginning, and I'm afraid some of the furniture got damaged."

Harris frowned. "How damaged?"

Shawn went through what had happened, and explained how the bed and settee had become shredded. Harris stared at them with a stern look, then his face lit up like a Christmas tree and he roared with laughter.

"I wouldn't have expected anything less from her to be honest. Don't worry about it."

Belle stared at her Alpha then at Shawn, not sure if she should be angry this had been planned, or surprised Shawn had made it work. Shawn sat back in his seat looking relieved as their Alpha continued to chuckle about the furniture. She then realized the role both Harris and Felix had taken in the plan. She decided there and then to forgive her Alpha, but Felix…well, she would still give him an arse kicking. She could get away with that.

Harris's laugher ebbed away. "I'm pleased you're back to yourself, Belle. Seeing you in that dark hole was tearing apart a lot of people who are fond of you. However, I am going to give you a warning. You are going to be my beta for a while. A person who this community *and myself,* needs to be able to approach and rely on. A beta is a person the community can turn to if I am busy, or away from the village. If you are unable to do this, then tell me now."

Belle shook her head, her heart picking up its pace. She realized just how close she was to losing the chance to be beta.

"I can do this, Alpha. I won't screw up, I promise."

He nodded. "Then the job is yours. Don't mess it up."

Belle blew a relieved breath out.

Felix came in at the end of the meeting to officially hand her the role. With Shawn watching in the corner, Belle and Felix grasped each other's forearm and looked toward their Alpha. Belle recited the words she'd practiced since being offered the post.

"I, Belle Grant, promise to uphold shifter law, to aid our Alpha by holding the spot of beta until Felix Rockwell returns to take his rightful place."

Felix and Belle's claws extended, and they both dug four of them into each other's skin just inside of the other's wrists. They then moved their arms so that their blood mixed, until the small pinpricks healed. Belle wasn't sure if it was her emotions or something else, but she was sure a zing went through her, and she gasped. She suddenly felt more in tune with the village. *Weird.*

Harris broke through her thoughts with a community-wide mental announcement. *"With my brother's departure, Belle Grant has temporarily taken his place as beta. Please don't bombard them with your tidings, there will be a party in the community hall tonight for you to do just that."*

"It's all up to you now," Felix said, patting her on the back. "Gotta look after this lunkhead, 'cause while I'm away things might go awry. I mean, he is supposed to be Alpha, but we all know who does the work around here."

Felix didn't even have a smirk on his face, he had said it with full seriousness. Belle laughed and looked toward Harris who stood shaking his head with a smile.

"You wish, little brother." Harris's expression changed, his smile fading. "But then one day this could be all yours."

Belle watched as Felix paled. "Nah, you're all right. I'm happy where I am, bro. Walker will take over when you get old and retire."

Belle swore she scented a tinge of fear coming from Felix. Was he worried he'd lose his brother? His parents had died when he was pretty young, and it was something he'd never really gotten over. Belle recalled in his teenage years how the boy had gone on several benders, punching other teens who *offended* him. Or he'd spent nights, even weeks, going on camping trips with the girls from the village. It was Harris, his *Alpha,* who gave him the space he needed before he had to take on his role as beta, as well as Harris in his role as brother-turned-parent who gave him the love he sought.

"I'm not going anywhere just yet, bro." Harris slapped his brother on the back affectionately. "Now I do believe we have to get ready for a party."

Felix whopped and left the room. "The tide awaits. Sex, sun, and more sex," he chanted down the hallway, passing Melinda, who was carrying a wriggling Walker and a large, white envelope.

Melinda gave Walker to his father and flapped the envelope. "When are you going to give it to him?" she asked.

"At the party."

"What are you giving him? I got him two boxes of condoms." Belle chuckled.

Harris snorted out a laugh. "That lad will need a factory of fucking condoms at the rate he goes at it."

"A little bit of traveling money," Melinda answered Belle's question. "He's done so well saving up, we thought it would be nice to double what he's got."

"Wow, that's like…"

"Yep." Melinda nodded with a smile on her face.

"He's going to have one bloody nice trip," Belle said. She knew full well Felix had saved a good couple of thousand.

* * * *

That night most of the village gathered in the town hall for Felix's going-away party. Felix had been saving for so long, adamant he was going out in the world before settling down. Belle thought it was very likely that he was going to see a whole lot more of naked women than the sights; that's why she'd bought him the condoms. He'd gone through the village females already.

By the end of the evening presents had been given to Felix, along with acknowledgments to Belle for now being beta. Belle was sure she'd seen a tear in Felix's eyes when Harris and Melinda gave him their gift. The love Felix had for his brother was as clear as the sun. Even though it was his brother who'd brought him up most of his life, there seemed to be no regrets. Both men hugged each other tight, ending in a lot of affectionate back slapping.

As for Belle's gift, Felix had laughed and tucked them into his rucksack.

"I'm glad I didn't get to shag you," he said, holding her in his arms.

"Oh really?" she asked, pretending to be heartbroken.

"Yeah, I would have spoiled it for your mate. Once you've had Felix, there's no going back."

They both laughed as a small growl could be heard behind them, coming from Shawn. Belle knew he wasn't really jealous of their friendship. he was just putting on a show. Felix pulled back from her and winked at Shawn.

Belle was tired. Turning around, she walked straight into her mate's arms and asked him to take her home. The last week was finally catching up with her.

Grabbing hold of her lifelong friend one last time before she left, she hugged him tight. "Take care out there, pussy cat. Call home a lot, right?"

"Aye aye." He winked, letting her go.

Without looking back Belle walked out of the building, silently wishing him to come home safe.

"He will be back," Shawn said, taking hold of her hand as they walked home.

"Yeah, I know. It's just he has been a friend for so long. I think a lot of the girls were jealous of our friendship. They tried so many times to have what I did with him. What they didn't know was I was the only one who didn't sleep with him. I didn't want his body, I just wanted to be his friend."

"I can't fill his space, but I will always be here when you need me." He pulled her tighter against him, his arm banding around her waist, halting their walk.

"You couldn't fill his space," she said, looking up and into his eyes, knowing full well what she was doing. He could do with a little winding up now and again. He needed to not take everything so seriously. Was that a little bit of panic she saw in his eyes? *Oops.* "You know why? Because I slept with you. I want more than just your friendship, my tiger, I want all of you," she added with a huge smile.

Chapter 23

"You, my tigress, are a minx. I certainly did sleep with you, and I intend to forever more." Shawn's lips clamped down over Belle's, leaving her breathless as he delved his tongue deep inside and made it dance with hers.

His hands roamed over her backside, and he kneaded her fleshy buttocks. A sudden slap had her squealing into his mouth.

"Mine." He grinned, then smacked his lips and licked them. "I suddenly feel awful hungry. I have a craving for some kind of rare honey."

Although she had a clue what he was up to, she wondered where he was going with this. He closed his eyes and breathed in deep and moaned.

"I can see it now, all wet and sticky, dripping from its pot." Shawn licked his lips again.

When he opened his eyes they burned with lust. Belle stepped back, somehow knowing that with this game he was playing, she was going to be running in a second.

"I'll put my fingers in and lick them first, then I'll use my tongue and lick the pot." He paused. "Why are you backing away from me, love?" he asked, his muscles tensing, ready for the chase that was about to begin.

"I'm not. I'm…umm… I am…" Fuck it, what was the word she was trying to think of? Why did those clear blue eyes that burned with a heavy dose of lust have her brain turning to mush and her body burning? Her pussy was also now dripping with the honey he spoke of, and her nipples were perky and poking out of the front of her top.

The grin on Shawn's face grew even wider. "Come here, little kitty."

His muscles tightened even more, and Belle could see he was ready to pounce. She'd show him. She pivoted on the spot and ran. She pushed herself as much as she could. Her muscles pumped, and her heart thundered. She could hear his footsteps behind her. She gained a little distance, but was sure that was just Shawn giving her time to run. He was enjoying himself. Seeing their house, she decided to take a slightly different route than just heading in the front door; hopefully it would give her the advantage of going somewhere he wasn't expecting.

She zipped to the right and took a barely walked path. The grass was flattened just enough for the mud to show the odd footprint or two. Jumping over a low wall, she then bounded over the wooden fence and into their back garden. She carried on running, a smile still on her face. If she was honest with herself, she enjoyed the game as much as Shawn did.

When fate put them together, it had certainly chosen right for her, and for him. She loved the man with all of her heart. The thought of losing him now… No, she couldn't think that. Was this how her mother and father had felt about each other? Did she have what they had? *Yes* was the only answer to that question.

At the bottom of the garden was a small clearing where her

parents would often sit and look over the village. It sat on a high enough peak that they could see most of Stonesdale. Arms banded around her hard enough that she misjudged her step. She couldn't lift her hands to protect herself from the ground as they were tightly held against her body. Shawn spun them around and he hit the ground and rolled so she lay under him, looking up into the sky.

"Gotcha." He lowered his head, and she found herself carried away with his heated kisses.

Her tongue dueled with his, and she savored the taste of her man. Spice and Shawn rolled into one. He pressed his engorged shaft against her jean-clad pussy. He was hot, hard, and ready. One of his hands clasped her butt while his other arm rested by her head, holding some of his weight off her, not that she minded. He was like a loveable, heated blanket on a cold winter's night that she didn't want to part with.

The hand on her butt moved as he kissed her neck. He unclasped her jeans button, pulled her zipper down, and slid inside. She shivered when a finger slipped through her damp folds and pressed against her throbbing clit.

"Oh!" Her hips bucked against his digit. Again he pressed then circled his finger around her clit. "Oh God," she cried out as he repeated the movements over and over. She swore the man was torturing her. She'd give him anything if only he made her come. "Pleeaase," she begged.

A bite to her neck and another hard press on her clit and her hips bucked, then her body froze for a few seconds and stars appeared as an orgasm flowed through her. Shawn's fingers delved inside of her pussy, and she could feel her slickness on his digits helping him enter her easily.

"Oh, my tigress, so hot, wet, and waiting for me. Do you want my cock?" he asked low and huskily near her ear.

She couldn't find her voice, but to moan. Shawn curled his fingers inside, hitting the most sensitive part of her. Another orgasm ripped through her.

"Please," she wailed again. "Please, Shawn, I can't... I..." She didn't think she could take another orgasm.

"Another one, Belle. Give me another and I'll fuck you here and now. I'll shove my cock deep inside you. I'll have you on your hands and knees, looking over the community you now help run. Do you want that, mate?"

She purred deep in her throat, her chest heaving with panting breath. Oh God, she wanted him inside her so much. His fingers were no match for his long, thick dick. His fingers kept running along her slick walls, her hips undulating, although she wasn't sure if it was for more or less. Pain and pleasure combined together.

"Now, please," she shouted. "Shawnnn!"

He bit down on his mark, and her whole body bucked underneath him as her pussy again clenched around his nimble fingers.

* * * *

Shawn watched his luscious mate twitch underneath him. Her face was peacefully sated, her eyes closed in bliss. She was flushed from her orgasms, and her chest rose and fell in small pants.

Pulling his fingers from her pussy, he licked them clean, moaning at her taste as it filled his mouth. Finally, clean, he moved his hand down and unbuckled his jeans, wincing slightly when his cock hit the air. Pre-cum already dotted the end of his shaft. He was eager to be inside her. Once he was free he lifted his mate up and rolled her over to her hands and knees. He smirked when she groaned at having to move. He had wanted to lick her honey, but now he was too eager to be inside her.

He'd given her three orgasms and loved watching her rock and scream throughout them. He needed to be inside her *now*, with an urgency. He settled himself over the top of her, and his mouth covered his mark and lapped at it. He could still taste the tang of blood in his mouth. His cock twitched. With one hand he placed his shaft at her entrance, and with his other hand on her hip, holding her securely, he closed his eyes as he entered her slowly.

"Oh, my tigress, I am forever yours. Your cunt is like home, welcoming and allll mine." He opened his eyes to watch himself withdraw. He groaned at the erotic sight of his cock soaked with her honey. He could feel his sex pulse.

Grabbing her hips with both hands, he thrust hard and fast inside her. His balls slapped against her clit. She pushed back at him and moaned. Lifting his right hand, he brought it down with an echoing slap against her butt. She cried out in pleasure and pushed back at him again. His kitty liked that. He did it again and again, making sure his slaps were in different positions on her backside so not to hurt or mark her too much.

Holding her hips again, he picked up his pace, thrusting deep, each time hitting the top of her cervix. She began meeting him thrust for thrust, and he watched her fingers curl into the earth below them. The cool air from the evening washed over his damp skin, and his breathing picked up. All around him the scent of nature mixed with the scent of sex. Small grunts mixed in with the deep purr coming from his chest. His orgasm was building, the tingling in his spine growing. He needed to get her off one more time. He wanted her pussy to grasp hold of his cock and milk it for all its worth.

"Fuck, baby!" he cried, so very close to losing it.

Moving his hand around her body, he found that hard, little bundle of nerves between her legs and circled it. She bucked harder, almost losing the pattern they'd created. She screamed out his name at the same time he roared. If he had to boast about something right then, it would be the fact he was fucking the village beta while looking over the community. That thought, though, stayed deep inside his mind.

* * * *

A month later

"Be home soon, babe. This meeting is taking forever." Belle sighed in his head.

He blew her a kiss and sent her a flow of love. Things had been going great for them. At first it had felt like a dream to Shawn. He couldn't believe his life had turned out as it had. When Belle had taken over as beta he'd been worried. He'd even had a few panic moments when Belle had come home in a bad mood. But not once had she been anything like Rosie. No matter what kind of day she'd had, she never once took it out on him. Yeah, she moaned and groaned, even to the point of snarling about her day sometimes, but she talked it through with him.

Belle had even commented how he was more relaxed, more at ease with everything. They had a unique companionship, which was helped by their tigers being able to talk to each other. If one was pissed, the other would find out why through their beast and, of course, rectify it. There was, however, a drawback to this uniqueness—their beasts were horny fuckers and would gang up together, getting more beast time out of Shawn and Belle. Well, at first they had, until the human side caught on to what the beast side was doing.

His work was brilliant too. Ben was a good man and had a lot of knowledge and stories about the village that Shawn loved to listen to. The old man was worried about his age and had spoken to Harris about it, informing him that if a new doctor wasn't brought in soon to take over, the community would be without one if anything was to happen to him. Harris had shaken his head at the man, telling him he was being silly and he would be there for another twenty to thirty years yet. But to satisfy him a new female doctor, who was a jaguar shifter, moved into the community and started to work with Ben on taking over slowly. She actually moved into Shawn's old place, new furniture included.

The new doc was pleasant enough and was welcomed into

the community like any other person. Shawn was worried in the beginning that Belle would get jealous he was working with another woman. But his mate showed no signs of concern. He knew he wouldn't touch anyone else with a barge pole, but things Rosie had said and done sometimes came to the forefront of his mind. Belle was always there to help him push them aside.

Shawn was currently sitting in what was quickly becoming his favorite spot—the small, green clearing in their back garden. He would often catch his mate sitting there, talking away to her parents, telling them about her day or week as if they were sitting with her.

They had also started to redecorate the house, turning the place into theirs. Shawn had even bought a new king-sized bed, hoping at some point Belle would stop thinking of the bedroom as her parents and instead as their own. It worked.

Two weeks ago, Belle discovered she was pregnant. It had been both a shock and yet somewhat expected, being they'd never used anything. Shawn didn't want the feel of latex between them, and Belle was happy with the knowledge that if a kit came along they would manage. She'd told him she wanted to fill the house up with the laughter of a family once again. They were already talking about how to decorate a room as a nursery.

Belle had informed Harris about the pregnancy a few days ago. She'd told him she was happy to hand the role of beta over to someone else if needed. But he was content for her to remain in the position, although he did tell her to take it easier.

Felix also kept in contact with everyone. He sent postcards

from every place he visited. Harris had even erected a huge notice board outside the post office where he stuck all the postcards for the community to read. For some reason Belle was the one who received the tales of his sexecapades. It seemed the man left a woman—or more—in every port with his stamp on them.

Shawn's world right now was awesome, but somewhere in the back of his mind, there was always Rosie. She was still out there, still free. Her two brothers with her.

Chapter 24

"*Shawn?*" Ben's voice interrupted Shawn's thoughts.

"*Yes, Doc?*"

"*We have a problem, It's Chris's son.*" Chris was one of the village enforcers. "*He's had a nasty accident, and I need to get him to the hospital in the city. Even with our healing there isn't anything I can do here. Both Harris and Belle are busy, and I can't interrupt them. So I thought of you.*"

Shawn started running toward the village surgery. For Ben to ask for his help *and* to take a shifter to the hospital, it was urgent. "*Glad to help. I'm on my way.*"

"*Thank you,*" he said, relief sounding in his voice. "*I phoned ahead, and an old shifter friend is waiting at the hospital for us.*" The doc carried on, filling Shawn in with what had happened.

Finally reaching the building, Shawn ran inside to see the pale face of Chris beside his unconscious son who was laying on a bed. The boy's right arm was covered from shoulder to fingers in a heavy bandage. Blood seeped through in spots.

"Glad you can help me," Ben said, coming up beside him. "The seats are laid down in the back of the jeep. Chris, can you lift Jake into the vehicle?"

Chris stood and looked warily at his son.

"It's okay," Ben comforted the man. "He's out for the count. You can't do any more damage to him just by picking him up. Well, unless you drop him on his arm, of course."

Chris bent over his son and lifted him up. Holding him as close to his body as he could, he carried him outside and placed him in the doc's jeep.

"Why didn't you call an ambulance, Ben?" Shawn asked.

"One, it would take too long for them to get here and then to explain when we can move him now. And two, shifter healing."

He didn't need to say any more. Shawn could only imagine with the boy's arm as busted up as it was, he was in for some pain. His bones would have to be reset before they could heal properly in their right positions. Shifters also tended to burn through meds faster than a human, which at times like this didn't help.

"What about the air ambulance?" Shawn asked. "You know it's an hour's drive at least."

The village was so far out in the sticks it was a long drive. If anything happened like this and someone needed hospital treatment fast, then normally the air ambulance was called out.

"Bad luck for the boy I'm afraid. The winds are pretty rough so no helicopters are flying tonight. That's why I sedated him, I knew it was going to be a trip and a half by land."

Crap. Getting into the driver's seat, Shawn started the engine. He could see the reluctance on Chris's face as he jumped into the passenger seat while Ben climbed into the back and fussed over Jake until he was happy the boy was comfortable. Once all were belted in Shawn drove toward the nearest hospital in West Morland.

A little over an hour later Shawn pulled up outside the

hospital. An old, white-haired doctor was waiting outside with a team of nurses. Throughout the trip Ben had called the doctor to let him know how far they were and the condition of the boy. Ben climbed out of the vehicle and shook hands with the doctor as they watched the nurses shift the boy from the jeep onto a gurney and then wheel him into the building. They followed after him with Chris beside them.

Shawn stood by the jeep, now alone. Now, as the adrenaline from the drive seeped out of his system, he realized he was standing in front of the hospital with no idea if he was to wait for the doc or not. *Shit.* He looked around in a panic as it suddenly hit him that this was the first time he'd been out of the village since Rosie had attacked him. The scents around him brought back memories of him waking up in the hospital.

Images flashed through his mind. Rosie screaming at him. Rosie hitting him. Rosie… Rosie… Rosie… His chest tightened. Why was he panicking now? It had been so long since he had felt like this. The world suddenly seemed a whole lot bigger. Being in the village had created a safe bubble for him to cope and live happily in. Now he was out in the big, wide world and Belle, his safe haven, was nowhere in sight.

Fuck! Come on, Shawn, pull yourself together. He bent over, his hands on his knees. He couldn't pull in a breath.

I here.

His tiger's deep, somber voice brought a small tad of calm, enough for him to fill his lungs. Shawn pushed another breath into his lungs and released it. After a few more it felt easier. The edges of his vision slowly lost their fuzziness.

I here, his tiger repeated, sending a flow of love and reassurance.

Thank you, old friend.

I tell you I not leave you again.

"*Shawn?*" Belle's voice broke through their conversation.

"*Oh shit. Fuck. I forgot to tell you. Shit, I am so sorry,*" Shawn rambled, a stream of curse words filling his side of the conversation in his mind. He was still in the midst of Rosie's memories. Panic, fear, and whatever else he'd gone through. He was automatically assuming Belle would be pissed he hadn't told her where he'd gone.

"*Are you okay? I came home and you weren't here. I only just got a report from Larry—I'm soo going to kick his arse tomorrow for the delay. I know where you are, don't fret. I was just worried about you.*"

Shawn calmed a little more. Belle wasn't mad at him. She wasn't shouting. She was calm. Taking another deep breath, he relaxed even more.

"*They've just taken Jake inside. Doc and Chris went with him. I'm standing here like a prat wondering what to do next.*" In his mind a small, hysterical laugh left him. "*Sorry. I panicked a little, and I feel kind of stupid.*"

"*Come home, my tiger, I'll be waiting for you.*"

He could feel her love. She sent him an image of them

entwined together. It made him feel even sillier for standing there panicking. She wasn't Rosie. She had never treated him as such either. Guilt now rolled through him.

Stop. She love you. You are hers, and she is yours.

Shawn sent his tiger a flow of love and thanks. Between his beast and Belle, Shawn felt stronger, and he pushed all the bad memories away.

"*I love you, my tigress.*"

"*I love you too, my tiger. Come home to me. I'll send Larry over to the hospital to wait for Ben and Chris. The fucker can do something useful.*"

Shawn drew in a breath and released it. His thundering heart slowly begin to beat normally. He brought an image into his mind of Belle, which calmed him even more. "*I'll be home as soon as I can. Thank you for being mine.*"

"*Drive safe. I'll be waiting.*"

Shawn climbed back into the jeep and started off for home. His mind was still in turmoil over panicking. Stupid fucking memories, they always hit him at unexpected times. Scents, sounds, sights all kicked them off. He'd thought he'd gotten over Rosie, but it seemed the woman had certainly left her mark on him.

The roads thinned out to single file country lanes as he neared the village. The day had been long, and he'd grown weary. Rolling down the window, he allowed the cool breeze to flow inside the jeep to help keep him awake. He came to a stop at the final junction before the last few miles toward home, and the hairs on his neck rose. He looked around. No other vehicles could be heard or were in sight. *Weird.* Perhaps he felt the heebie-jeebies because he was tired.

He had placed his foot on the accelerator to cross the junction when from out of nowhere he caught sight of a moving shadow to his right. Slamming on the brakes, he again looked around. Seeing nothing, he shook his head. Perhaps he was more physically drained than he thought. A scent carried in from the wind prickled his nose. He looked back out of the windscreen and there in the middle of the road stood Rosie. *Fuck, fuck, fuck!*

"No, no, no. You're seeing things, Burr," he told himself aloud. "You're more tired than you feel. Drive, man. Drive. Get home and into the arms of your mate. She always makes things better."

It her. I can smell her evil scent. Drive or let me eat. His tiger growled low. *I eat even if she make me sick,* his tiger added.

His animal pushed at him underneath his skin. Claws racked across the inside his stomach, and fur started rippling over his skin. Even though Shawn was frozen with fear, he had just enough sense to place his foot back onto the accelerator.

"Don't even think about it, you fucking pansy."

Shawn recognized that voice. It was David, one of Rosie's brothers. Shawn assumed by the press of metal against his temple, the man had a gun.

Let me out. Let me eat, his tiger growled deep in his mind, pushing further at him to be released.

No, my friend, please. He could kill you...us. Be patient. You will *get your time, I promise.*

You better. His tiger pulled back, but remained on alert.

Shawn placed his foot back on the brake. The passenger door opened and another of Rosie's brothers, Paul, climbed into the jeep. He too had a gun in his hand.

"Get in the back," he ordered, pulling the hand-brake up.

Shawn opened the driver's door and climbed into the back just as Rosie did the same on the other side.

"Hello, lover," Rosie sneered.

Remembering about her injuries Shawn looked her over carefully. She no longer had any sign of the injuries that he had supposedly created. She actually looked good, even though she was on the run.

"It's about time you left that fucking village. We couldn't risk getting near you while you were in there. Little villages have a lot of eyes."

Shawn finally came out of his daze. Rosie...Rosie was sitting next to him.

"How did you know where I was?" He'd believed he was safe in Stonesdale. No one but the police knew where he was.

Rosie laughed. "Oh, we have a friend who believed my story." Her eyes filled with tears, her face changing to someone who was in pain. She even started wrapping her fingers around each other, like someone afraid to be where they were. "He hit me all the time," she wailed. "He was always telling me I was fat and I should lose weight. I had to keep my job even though I hated it…"

She let the sentence trail off and looked at him, her whole demeanor changing to one of a predator instead of a victim. Even Shawn thought she'd looked convincing.

"You remember the nice detective Johnathon? He told me where you were, said my brothers might like to know. Wasn't that kind was of him?" she asked, her voice all smug again.

Shawn knew the man didn't like him, but to do this? After he got out of this—if he did—he would make sure he filed a complaint about the man.

"Why are you doing this?" He wanted to tell her to let him go, that he didn't love her and she didn't love him. He just wanted to live his life and put her in the past.

"You told the police, you fucking moron. They came after me! What the fuck did you do that for? I loved you, Shawn. I gave you everything. A car, a home. All you had to do was do as you were told," Rosie screamed at him, spit flying from her mouth as she spoke.

"I'll take it back. I'll tell them I lied. Just please let me go. If you loved me like you say, let me go."

Rosie shook her head, a look of disgust on her face. "You don't get it, do you? I made you. You belonged to me. This Belle?" She sneered. "Is she your new fuck mate? A new lover? She likes sloppy seconds, does she? Well, guess what, if I can't have you, she can't either." Rosie turned toward the front and ignored him.

Shawn knew he couldn't risk shifting with a gun pointed at

him. Shifter healing wouldn't help if he was dead.

David climbed into the driver's seat and pulled away from the junction. Not in the direction of Stonesdale either. Shawn knew he was in big trouble. He had a small advantage though; he was a shifter who could talk mentally to other shifters, no matter the distance.

"*Belle,*" he called out.

Suddenly, he felt pain on the side of his head, caused by something coming from Rosie's side of the car, and it had him closing his eyes tightly. Bile rose from his stomach as nausea rocked through him. Rosie had hit him? Yeah, that was normal.

He managed to open his eyes briefly before the darkness pulled him under, and his only thought was Belle. "*I love you, my tigress.*"

Chapter 25

"Wakey, Wakey, sleepyhead." A shrill voice broke through his sleep.

"Belle?" Shawn's voice came out gruff. He tried to raise his hand to his face, but he couldn't move it. *Huh?*

Questions filled his thoughts. What day was it? Why was his bed hard, and who the hell was talking to him? He could smell perfume, wood, and dirt all rolled into one. Belle didn't wear perfume. In fact, no shifter did, because it messed with their senses.

"Nope. Open your eyes, fucker." A deeper voice had him opening his eyes. Nausea rolled through him as he did. He swallowed repeatedly until it dissipated.

"Finally!" said the shrill voice he'd heard earlier.

It all came back to him. Rosie!

Shawn looked around quickly. He was in what looked like an abandoned house. Paint was scraped off the woodwork. Old yellow wallpaper curled at the edges. Ropes were tied around his wrists, and from what he could tell his ankles too. He was sitting in a chair in front of a small table. Around it sat Rosie and her two brothers. Two guns lay on the table between them. The room they were in had sleeping bags in the corners. On the kitchen counter he could see an old camp stove with pans and cups strewn around it. It looked like the family had been camping there for a while.

He couldn't hear any traffic outside, just the occasional bird chirping, so maybe they hadn't brought him back to the city. How the fuck was he going to get out of this? The sun was shining through boards nailed to the windows, so he knew he'd been there overnight at least.

Belle…he had to tell Belle or Harris where he was; perhaps they could help him.

"Where are we?" he asked.

All three of them laughed.

"You think we would have knocked you out if we wanted you to know? Stupid fucker," David said, shaking his head. "What you go get with a dunce for?" he asked his sister.

"Shut up. I can't say much for your wife," Rosie bit back.

Instead of blowing up at Rosie, David nodded his head and laughed. "Yeah, you got me there. I went back for some money last week and she tried to hide it from me. Stupid bitch. I showed her."

Shawn tuned them out, trying to think of a way to get out of this mess.

I here still. Release me, I'll show them. Guns aren't in their hands now.

I'm glad you're with me, old friend. I'm not sure we could shift quick enough. I need to find out where we are.

I tell our mate. She tell Alpha. They coming.

Shawn's heart picked up a beat. He'd forgotten his tiger was able to talk to Belle's. *They don't know where we are.*

When you sleep, I tell mate directions car took. They scent the rest.

Oh God, he could actually get out of this alive. He sent a

huge flow of love to his beast. Never in his life, not even when he was a teenager, had he not loved his tiger. When his beast had stopped talking to him before because of his relationship, he'd been heartbroken. It seemed his feline was making up for things now.

I tell you I never leave again.

Before he could send a message to Belle, Rosie brought him out of his thoughts and conversation with his tiger by slapping a hand around his face. He couldn't even raise his own hand to the burn.

"I asked you a fucking question! Don't zone out on me," she ordered. "We need you to write a statement saying you falsely accused me of stabbing you. Will you do it?"

Shawn realized that although he was afraid of the situation he was in, he wasn't actually afraid of the woman sitting beside him anymore. She'd spent years abusing him, physically and mentally, and he'd spent those years afraid and walking on eggshells. Now, though, as he looked at her, he didn't feel afraid of her. She just looked like an average woman he'd meet on the street. Someone that he probably wouldn't even notice since he'd met Belle.

Belle had helped him heal. Yes, he still had panic moments, but they were becoming less and less frequent. He was going to be a father; he had to live. The thought of Belle hurting because he'd died broke his heart. No, he had to get out of this.

He looked into the eyes of his former fiancée. He didn't love this woman anymore. He didn't even hate her. He pitied her more than anything else, plus any man she loved in the future.

"Belle," he called out in his mind. Rosie could wait for his answer a bit longer.

"Oh, my tiger. I was so worried, but your beast kept talking to mine and we are nearly there with you. Are you hurt?"

"Only my pride so far." He tried to mentally chuckle, but it came out a little limp. She was near. His mate had come for him. Shouldn't it be the other way around? It was time he took this situation and turned it around. Another slap brought him out of his thoughts.

"For fuck's sake! I'm going to shoot you myself," Rosie screamed at him.

No hit no more. Enough! his tiger roared inside of him.

Instead of holding his beast back, Shawn pulled back in his mind and gave his body over to his tiger. Shawn opened his mouth and roared; it mixed in with Rosie's scream of terror filling the small room. Orange and black fur slid out of Shawn's pore. His fangs grew. His body changed. His clothes ripped, some of the material falling to the floor. The ropes that had been holding him down frayed and broke string by string, until finally his beast stood on all fours, growling at the three pathetic people in the room. His feline shook himself free from the rest of Shawn's clothes.

"What the fuck? What the fuck, man?" David screamed, scrabbling backward. His chair went flying behind him, banging against the floor. The man looked as white as a ghost. His lips moved in silent prayer.

"Shiiiiiiiiiiit," Paul yelled. He kicked the table as he moved backward, and the guns went sprawling.

Too scared to shoot. His tiger chuckled, licking his lips for show.

The average weight for his kind of tiger was about eight hundred and fifty pounds, but for a shifter, their body mass was bigger. Shawn chuckled mentally, watching the three people who'd kidnapped him and probably had plans to make him disappear, cower in fear in front of a nine hundred pound tiger.

"Did you know he could do that?" David asked his sister with a shaky voice. His hands were held up in a surrender motion to the tiger.

Shawn's feline roared, hating the sound of the male's voice. If Shawn could have laughed out loud, he would have, but instead he happily sat back in their shared mind and mentally laughed.

"Shawn?" Belle's wonderful voice filled his mind. *"My tiger says her mate is free. Are you okay?"*

"He's free all right. The three of them are cowering at the moment. I'm not sure for how long though. I can't see the guns that went flying."

All of a sudden the battered front door to the abandoned property went flying to the floor with a resounding bang. A white and black striped, huge, growling tiger came bounding into the room. A large snow leopard and cougar prowled in after her.

"Honey, I'm home," Belle quipped.

Her feline vaulted over the fallen table and chairs straight to him. Both of the cats' heads butted gently with each other in affection. A lot of rubbing against each other came after, both of them eager to spread their scent on their mate. Shawn's cat wanted to fuck his mate there and then. He acted as if he hadn't seen her in ages.

"Hey you two, business now, fuck later," Harris warned them.

Shawn's feline snorted, but paid attention. Belle's cat turned to the cowering threesome and growled deep and low. The pungent smell of urine drifted their way.

"What are we going to do with them?" Shawn asked.

The snow leopard suddenly shifted, leaving a naked Harris standing in its place. Rosie's mouth opened in shock, but then she smiled, apparently liking what she saw. Shifters were never really concerned about being nude, it was kinda normal to them. Belle followed suit, shifting into her human form, Shawn after. The cougar, however, stayed in his cat form. Harris picked up a fallen chair and sat on it. Belle again followed suit.

"What the fuck are you?" David asked, quivering in fear.

The cougar stepped forward and yowled.

David's eyes popped open more in fear. "Oh God, is he going to eat me?"

Harris laughed. "No, you would probably make him sick."

Shawn moved behind Belle and placed a hand on her naked shoulder. He looked over at Rosie, making it known Belle was his now.

"You freak," she screamed and dived off the floor toward him.

Belle was up on her feet and in front of Shawn in a flash. Rosie immediately lifted her hands to place them around Belle's neck, but Belle knocked them out of the way and then pushed at the screaming woman's shoulders, a deep, low growl coming from Belle's throat. Rosie landed on the floor with a bump and a groan. She tried getting back up, but Belle's bare foot stomped on her stomach.

"You will never touch him again, bitch. He is mine now."

"He's just sloppy seconds," Rosie sneered.

Belle turned to look at Shawn, a huge smile on her face. "Sloppy? Only when his cum is dripping from my pussy. Seconds? No, always my first and forever."

He couldn't help but take a step over to her and slide his hands into her hair and kiss her.

"I missed you, my tiger," she said.

"As I did you, my tigress." He pulled his hands from her hair and slid them around her waist.

"Nooo," Rosie screeched again. "I made him."

Belle pressed on her stomach again, shutting the woman up. She lay still and whimpered.

"What are you going to do to us? What are you?" moaned Paul. "Our brothers know where we are and will come looking for us."

"We are your worst nightmare." Harris leaned forward in his chair. "However, we don't intend to kill you, although in a few years you'll wish we had." Harris stood and grinned. "That doesn't mean we're letting you go."

Shawn's cat let out a disappointed yowl in his head. He wondered himself what they were going to do with them. If they weren't letting them go free, and they'd seen their cats, what did Harris have planned for them? He was about to ask when he heard two cars drive up and park. He tensed until he scented his own kind. Larry, Henry, and another enforcer, Mark, stepped into the house carrying clothes.

"Ready when you are, Alpha. No one around but us," Mark said and stepped back outside.

Harris took two pairs of jogging pants from Henry, handing one of them to Shawn. Terry, who was the cougar shifter, remained in his animal form. Belle was handed a white shirt.

Shawn was more than a little confused now. What were they intending to do with Rosie and her brothers? He looked at Harris. His Alpha smirked back.

Chapter 26

"We did a little digging and found out it's not only Rosie who likes to abuse her partner. Her brothers are guilty of it too. Each of them has a wife or girlfriend in bad ways. So we decided to make the family disappear. That way no one will ever again be hurt by any of them." Harris turned toward the three siblings who were currently having their hands and feet handcuffed together. "About now, another team of my enforcers are picking up your three brothers. You are all going to be placed in wooden crates and shipped off to a friend of ours way up north. There is a small clan of wolves up there who live further from humanity than any other shifters I know of. They live in harsh conditions and love it. Strange but true. You will be joining them."

"You can't do this. My wife will go straight to the police if I don't come home."

Harris snorted and lifted David to his feet. "When you don't return home for seven years you will be declared dead. At that time, your wife will receive a substantial amount of money you left her in a will."

"That's bull. It's her fucking loss too. I don't have any money and definitely no fucking will. I wouldn't leave her any fucking thing, even if I did have money."

"You do now. Or should I say there will be."

Each of the siblings were lifted off the floor and made to jump outside. Two vans were parked outside, and when the doors were opened Shawn could see three wooden crates, each one just big enough for one person to fit inside.

"No. No, you can't do this," Rosie screeched at Shawn. "You fucking wanker, I'll get you for this. I gave you everything, you tosser."

Larry, who was the one holding the screeching woman, pulled a syringe out of his jacket pocket. Removing the cap with his teeth, he pushed the needle in Rosie's arm. A couple of minutes later, she dozed off, and she was shoved into a crate, as were her brothers.

"They are really heading for slave labor?" Shawn asked his Alpha.

"Yes. They will work hard for the rest of their lives. They won't harm anyone ever again."

Shawn winced a bit, and Harris must have spotted it.

"It's either this, Shawn, or we kill them. They've seen who we are," he said, climbing into one of the vans alongside Belle and Shawn.

"But what if they get free?"

"They won't," Harris growled. "Believe me, they won't."

"What if they are seen or something if a human visits the clan?" Shawn asked.

Harris snorted. "Where they're going, the clan only receive deliveries twice a year. They won't be seen by a human ever again."

"Thank you," Shawn said with his heart in his mouth. No matter what Rosie and her family had done, he didn't want them to die. Maybe this was a better thing to happen to them. "From the bottom of my heart, I could not thank you enough."

"You don't have to, son, just look after your mate and we will be fine."

Shawn looked toward Belle. "There will never be a day that passes that I won't love her." He pulled his mate onto his lap as the van pulled away from the house and kissed her like there was no tomorrow. He had been so worried he would never see her again.

"I'm here, my tiger."

"I can't wait to get you home."

"Me either."

* * * *

"I love you, my tigress."

Shawn's words circled around in Belle's mind. The words had been a whisper in her mind. When she couldn't contact him after that, she'd asked her cat to get in contact with her mate. For some bizarre reason, fate had deemed it necessary that their cats be able to talk to each other. Maybe this was just that reason.

After she'd informed the Alpha of Shawn's situation, plans had quickly been made and put into action. The community had a huge warehouse on the outskirts of the village, it was there six wooden crates were picked up and loaded into two vans.

Although Belle agreed with Harris's plan, her cat had strongly disagreed with it. She wanted to bite their heads off, especially the evil female who had hurt her mate. The time it had taken them to get to where Shawn had been taken was horrible.

She'd imagined finding all kinds of things when she got there. Thoughts of losing her mate so soon after her parents hurt her heart. But hearing his voice, then her cat telling her that her mate was free had her breathing a sigh of relief. It was even better seeing her mate once the front door was down.

Now there she was curled up with her mate on the way home. She buried her nose into his neck and licked over her mark.

"If you keep doing that, my tigress, our Alpha and your fellow enforcer will see you placed on all fours while I fuck you."

Belle's cheeks filled with heat, and she pulled her head back from his neck. "You wouldn't," she dared.

He smiled as he wiggled his eyebrows, and she knew he would.

"You're a bad man."

"Does that turn you on?" he asked, his voice lowering.

"Wait 'til you get home. I don't really wish to see my beta being bent over and fucked. Especially in my car," Harris warned from the front.

Belle blushed again, and Shawn grinned from ear to ear. Her Alpha was one hell of a cock blocker.

"Have you heard anything from Chris about his boy?" Shawn asked.

"Aye, not long ago actually," Harris said, looking in the rearview mirror. "Jake came through the operation really well. He will have to wear a cast for a few days. Chris said the doctor was fucking amazing. He managed to mend his boy's arm without having to add any implants. Implants would have made the boy's shifting days hard, if not impossible."

That was a shifter's nightmare. If any kind of foreign body had to be inserted for some reason, it could get in the way for the changing of bones and muscles.

"Excellent." Shawn grinned. "When will he be coming home?"

Harris laughed. "Tomorrow if Jake has his way. He's already moaning about being there."

The rest of the trip was extremely hard. Belle's tiger kept sending her naughty images. When they reached the edge of the village, Belle asked Harris to stop the car, and she couldn't get out quick enough. Shawn hastily followed her, and they had both stripped and shifted before Harris even pulled away. Both tigers ran, each of them eager to re-kindle with each other. Belle's cat loved the chase, but she liked being caught more.

* * * *

It was a good hour later before the cats were relaxed and sated enough for Belle and Shawn to claim their human forms. Shawn pulled her into the house and up the stairs to the shower. His hands never left some part of her body. They touched the small of her back when she walked, they held her shoulders as he kissed her before entering the shower. They roamed over her naked, damp skin as the water rained down on them both.

"I thought I would never see you again," he confessed.

"When you whispered you loved me, I was so scared.

Nothing can happen to you, Shawn, our kit is going to need his or her father."

"You heard me telling you I loved you?"

"Yeah, it came through as a whisper."

"The darkness was pulling me under, and my last thought was I needed to tell you I loved you."

Standing on her tiptoes, Belle reached up to kiss him. Shawn's hands drifted down and under her buttocks. With a quick raise he lifted her into his arms. His mouth was over hers in a flash. His tongue met hers and they slid over each other. Their moans sang out together.

Her hands drifted up and into his wet hair, the strands slipping through her fingers. All thoughts of never seeing him again drifted away. She relaxed, knowing he was safe and sound in her arms. Their light kisses grew heavier, and Shawn nudged his cock against her clit. She groaned.

One of his hands kneaded one of her breasts, and he ran a finger over its peaked nipple. Then two fingers rolled the bud. Nerve endings filled with small shocks that ran down her body to her clit. Shawn bucked his hips again, and her tiny bundle of nerves ran along his rigid shaft.

"Oh!" she cried.

She needed more. He seemed to sense that and his hand moved down in between them and one of his nimble fingers ran a circle around her nub then pressed on it. It was her turn to buck her hips. She climbed his body, wrapping her legs around his waist. Her arms banded around his neck, holding on fiercely.

"Don't ever leave me again," she begged.

"Never." He licked over his mate mark, causing another shock to travel through her body, straight to that tiny bundle of nerves between her legs. Two of his fingers entered her and withdrew. "So wet and willing and ready for me," he huskily whispered into her ear.

She actually heard herself whimper at the loss of his digits. The emptiness didn't last long. He lined up his cock, and she gasped as he entered her quick and fast. Her back hit the tiles behind her.

"This will be hard and fast," Shawn warned. "I missed you, my tigress."

He began thrusting just as he'd said he would—hard and fast. His sex was so thick she could feel every single ridge as they moved against the walls of her pussy. Her breasts were tightly pressed against his chest.

Her orgasm built quickly, and it wasn't long before he plunged into her and froze, his roar echoing around the bathroom and his cock jerking its seed into her womb. She burned from the inside out, and lights flashed behind her eyes. Her heart thundered, and her breath froze in her lungs. She kissed her mate with more passion that she'd ever possessed.

Pulling back, she started into Shawn's blue eyes and saw the love that her parents had. She had what she'd always wanted. It all came back and hit her; for a brief time she thought she'd lost him. Tears began blinding her.

"I was so close to losing you. Never again. Promise me," she pleaded. Her chest felt so tight with fear. She blamed it on her hormones, because normally she wasn't one to cry. But thinking that she'd almost lost him forever…well, she had a right to cry, didn't she?

"Sweetheart, you and I will sit in our tiger forms and watch the sun set and rise over the village for years to come."

He kissed the end of her nose and reached behind her to turn the water off. He then wrapped her in a huge, fluffy towel and carried her to their bed.

"I'm going to make love to you now. Just a small reminder of what we have to look forward to for the next hundred or so years. I'm so glad I found you. You helped me heal, you gave me a kit, a family, and a life worth living for."

Tears again flooded her eyes. Who would have believed fate could hand her such a generous, kind-hearted, handsome man? She was going to make sure no one ever hurt him again. She would give him his happily ever after.

Printed in Great Britain
by Amazon